Dedication

This book is dedicated to my family, for all of the love and support they have given to me for many years. Just remember you can do anything, if you set your mind to it. All things are possible with our Lord God.

Romans 14:11
For it is written: "*As* I live, says the Lord, Every knee shall bow to Me, and every tongue shall confess to God."

Introduction

This is a book of writings that were written of the remembrances of times past. Within these are a little truth, a little fiction and hopefully a little humor. With guidance from our Lord and the love of my family, I hope you are able to relate to and enjoy some of these.

Our God wants us to learn from our experiences and the things we sometimes ponder about in our minds while thinking back on those events in our lives. Yes, the Lord does have a sense of humor. With that being said just look in the mirror.

About the Author
Don Pierce

My wife and I live in a small town, which is located in the southwestern area of the state of Michigan. This is my first book written on the remembrances of times past. Over the course of my life I have had the experience of living in various places within the United States.

Please note that these small writings, are written with a little truth, a little fiction, and hopefully some humor for you to enjoy. With this book, I hope the Lord brings back a memory which you have enjoyed over the time of your life. One of these may even bring a smile to your face.

Table Of Contents

Dedication
Introduction
About the Author
Table Of Contents

1 Seasons Of Change

As I look outside at the cold February day, it came across my mind of the upcoming time of spring just around the corner with all of the flowers, rain, sunshine and even the bugs that go along with it. Shortly after that comes the beginning of the summer season and Memorial Day. How the seasons change quickly in our lives. When I was young I could hardly wait for something to change. Even today without me knowing, things are changing all around me.

With the change of summer coming, I think back at the time when I was young and there were still a lot of my older family members around and we would pack up the car and head down south to visit them. That was always a fun time to hang out with cousins and other family members. Of course there was always a little mischief going on when we got all of the cousins together. In a small town where all of our relatives were from, everybody knew everybody and you could not get by with too much. We would play outside all day and then chase the fireflies before being made to come in at night. Some of the years we would spend the whole summer at our grandparents. What a change it was staying with my grandparents (WOW!).

One of the traditions that we did down south was honoring our past family members and war veterans at the cemetery on Memorial Day. All of the ladies would have several dishes packed up in the picnic baskets. My uncle George would bring the # 3 wash tubs loaded with ice and cold pop. Down south they call it soda. Everybody would also bring rakes, shovels, flowers, etc. These would be used by all to clean up the grounds and plant flowers after the winter season. Back then, no matter how old you were, if you could walk, you could rake. As the work on the family grave sites would start to come to an end, the ladies would start setting up the food for dinner. Of course Uncle George would have to sample a soda from one of the wash tubs to make sure they were still cold enough.

A short period of time before we would say grace over the food my great grandfather would have all of us and the cousins gather around him and take a walk through the family grave markers and tell us things about each person and their relation to all of us. When it came to my great grandfather you had better listen the first time, because he was the kind of man that was tough as leather. From past experience, it was not pretty if you did not listen the first time he said something. (Hold on a second, I just had a flash back of how I loved my great grandmother's homemade musky dime jelly.) After our family history lesson it was time to eat.

When our family meal was over the adults would have a social time and the children would play some kind of ball, tag, or even hide and seek in the cemetery, until it was time to leave. As I ponder in my mind about this season in my life, I think what is God leaving me with i.e. of this old southern tradition? God gave us His Son to make a change in our lives. There have been many changes in the seasons of my life. What changes in my life do I need to do, which leads me in the direction that the Lord wants me to go? So to sum it up, in our lives there will be changes like the seasons. Are we willing to make that change and cleanup the cemetery grounds like the old southern tradition? Or will be left to wonder where the seasons went?

2 Hammer And Nails

Can you believe that it is spring already? For this fellow it did not come quick enough this year. All I can say about that, is the Lord must be working on me with my patience issues I sometimes have. With the warmer weather it reminds me of the fruit trees starting to bud. The grass starting to turn green and all of the bugs coming out.

With that being said it also reminds me of a time in my teenage years when one spring while being home and helping with preparing the ground, planting, and getting the one acre garden ready, there was that special project that dad would plan for us four boys to work on. It seemed like he always had that little project for us all to do. The project for the spring of 1973 was the new dry well. In case you did not know what a dry well is, it is an underground drainage system to take excess water away from the house, which helps with the prevention of flooding.

Now if you knew my dad, he was a quiet man and he only liked to tell us boys one time. So in other words you had better listen to him closely the first time, because the second time was not pretty. He also was the kind of person that once you did the job, do it right and do it so that it would last. One example of that is when he had central air put in the house the installer said that a 1 horse power motor would be sufficient for the home, he told them to make sure to put in a little bigger motor at a 1 ½ horse power.

Well back to the dry well project. The night before dad had told us he wanted all of us home on that coming Saturday morning to start the project. He had marked off a spot in the back yard for the new dry well. He had even bought a couple of new shovels. Of course early that Saturday morning he had come upstairs and woke us up, reminding us that we were burning daylight and it was time to start digging. Of course with dad when it came to the size of that dry well I think it would have been big enough for three homes. From time to time mom would bring us out cold water and ice tea. One thing that our mother would do is always ask us, where dad was so she could take him a cold drink too. She made sure that we had a good solid lunch the days we were digging the hole and trenches. Of course dad would follow up on us, serval times making sure that we were doing it to the specs he wanted. It sure seemed like it took us a month of Sundays to dig that dry well and all of the trenching.

As I get older and remember some of the projects we did as kids, I came to the realization that my parents were Hammerin' Nails in our foundation. A good builder knows that before you can lay a brick you need a good foundation and a sturdy wall. My dad would do this in ways like making us listen closely the first time, getting an early start on the task at hand, making sure that the work is done well and more than sufficient. My mom was doing this by setting an example of how a wife and mother should take care of her children and husband.

In relating this to my life as a Christian, I think of how Jesus is Hammerin' Nails in my foundation through reading his word, attending church, teaching me how to watch over my wife, family, etc. With the spring and Easter service reminding me again how Jesus literality took the Hammerin' of Nails in His body, so that I would have that everlasting foundation with Him. He died and rose for me, my family, and all of us. A question I have, are we allowing Jesus the opportunity for Hammerin' Nails in our foundation?

3 Mountain Dew

As the dog days of summer are upon us I can remember a time back when I was twelve years old. It was one of those summers when we went down to Arkansas to visit the grandparents, and spend our summer vacation from school with them. The part of Arkansas that we went down to, was in the Delta area where they raised a lot of cotton and rice. It was always hot down south. This summer was one of those that in the morning at 5:30 a.m., the temperature would be pushing over ninety degrees. It would be so hot that when you took a bath your hair seemed like it would never dry all day. Of course when your twelve years old the heat really did not bother you that much. My grandparents did not have a television at that time. The video games were not invented and you did not want to hang around the house or you would have been put to doing some major work of some kind. It was all about going outside and playing with your cousins and friends and trying not to get into very much trouble. Of course sometimes it seemed like trouble would find us.

This summer would be a little bit different, than the all of our other times when our parents, dropped us off for our summer vacation from school. That was the year that the soda pop Mountain Dew was coming to the market. They had chosen our little town in Arkansas as one of the testing areas to see how the public would accept the new brand called Mountain Dew. They had big signs in the grocery stores, along with a special program they were doing with the local movie theater. The promotion with the movie theater was, on Saturday mornings they would show a movie to the kids. These were movies like the Lone Ranger, Roy Rogers, etc. At the theater they would have drawings for free prizes to be given away to the kids that attended the show. The cost of getting into the movie was six soda bottle caps that came from the Mountain Dew pop. This was the only way you could get into the theater was with those six little caps. Once you got into the movie you held onto your ticket stub like it was a lump of gold. The prize drawing would be after the show was over. The prizes they would give away were things like hats with the Mountain Dew logo, kites, dolls, six packs of Mountain Dew soda, etc. Of course

8

the number one big prize that every boy there wanted was that Daisy BB gun.

All that summer the hunt was on, for getting those bottle caps. When it came to those metal caps we would pull out all of the stops. It seemed like we would ask our grandparents to pick us up some Mountain Dew soda at the store. Of course that did not happen too often. We would ask for paying work around the house. I think that my grandfather had the cleanest car in that whole town, maybe the whole county that summer. We would get up early every day and go hunting for those priceless bottle caps. We would also go looking for paying work that would give us some money to buy that Mountain Dew. We would walk around town looking for those bottle caps at the gas stations and other places that had outside soda machines. Back then most of your pop machines had a bottle opener on the outside of the machine, or an open box were the caps would drop in, when you opened the bottle. We would also look in the parks and other public places in the town for those golden tops. Needless to say, I was not the only one that was looking for the caps but all of the other kids in town. It seemed that that movie house was filled every Saturday morning for the Mountain Dew promotion. By the end of the summer those precious bottle caps were hard to come by. Every once in a while you would run across a young fellow with a black eye. A big percentage of the time that black eye came over those Dew caps.

As I reflect on this time, I think how I can apply this, to my Christian walk today. Am I willing to get out in the heat of the day to witness for the Lord? Am I motivated to work in doing His will? Am I seeking the number one prize of His grace? Will I be able to take that black eye for Him? So when you go on that summer hunt with your cowboy hat on, and your six gun by your side, remember the Lord will make a way for you to find those (lost ones) caps to win the prize.

4 Harvest Canning

It was a warm summer morning and we were home canning up some fresh corn off of the cob. With the weighted pressure canner being hot, the steam was rolling out of the area of the weight, while it was making that hissing sound. The little weight was jiggling, and dancing like a jumping bean from the pressure and the steam escaping. All of this took me back to another one of those times when we would visit my grandparents down south. Of course down south away from the Michigan winters your summer was long enough to grow two seasons of a garden.

With those two seasons it seemed like my grandparents would have their pressure canner going all of the time. I can remember that my grandparents had a small back porch attached to the back of the house. It was completely screened in and you had to go through it to go outside from the back door. On this porch there was big cook stove along with a sink, freezer and plenty of kitchen cabinets. This was my grandmothers outside kitchen used for putting up food from the garden. It only made sense, to have a setup on a porch like this due to some of extreme heat of the summers down in the delta part of the south they lived in. One day when we were down for a visit and I was inside getting into trouble with my grandfather, he directed to go outside and play. Well when grand dad told you to do something, you had better move fast and get it done or you paid a price, if you know what I mean. Yes back in those days you did not sit inside and play video games, watch a sixty five inch color HD television. You were lucky to even have a television, so the only entertainment you had is what you made. Oh yeah don't even think about messing with gramps prize banana tree in the yard. That is another story.

As I was going outside to play, through the back door I noticed a monster of an item, on my grandmothers stove on the back porch. This item was a double decker pressure canner. It was the old school type, that when you put on the lid, you had about six wing nuts you had to tighten down. It looked like it was so big that it would take two men and a small boy to move it. With my curiosity peaked, I asked my grandmother what it was and she proceeded to explain and tell me all about, what this monster of a beast is used for. She gave me a detailed lesson on that pressure canner and how to use it. Of course to a ten year old the fun part of the lesson was when she said, she had a friend that was using her canner and it blew up in her kitchen. I also liked the part when she said that the fish cakes we had last night, for supper, were from her canning up some fish with that pressure canner, that my grandfather had brought home. While setting at the table loaded with fresh canned tomatoes I heard something pop. The first thought that went through my mind was, is the pressure canner going to blow up. I asked my grandmother if she heard that pop. She answered yes and said grandson it was music to her ears for another jar had properly sealed itself. After about a half hour of the lesson and sweating in the heat of the outdoor screened in kitchen, I was ready to go outside. I was surprised she did not put me to work doing something in the kitchen. As I went outside I saw that my gramps was working in the garden and hoeing out some of the weeds. I made a hard right and went into the woods to avoid being detected for fear of winding up working in the garden. My grandparents were not afraid of assigning some kind of home chores to you. I often heard my grandfather say, if you can walk, you can work, so get to it.

At the sound of our pressure canner going and I think back on this time, I wonder what lesson the Lord has for me through this. Is the Lord reminding me, to be prepared for the day of His coming? Am I putting up treasures in heaven for Him? Do I try to avoid the work He has set before me? Will my life blow up without Him involved in my daily walk? Like my grandmother said, with Jesus by my side and I hear that pop of the jar sealing, it will be music to my ears.

5 Finding A Nut

I was in the kitchen getting a cup of coffee and looking out one of the windows. A squirrel was in the middle of the yard digging a hole to bury a nut for the winter storage. It came to me that was what my wife and I would be doing, in a little while, by home canning some green beans that were freshly picked the day before. It is wonderful how the Lord had given that squirrel and I the same mindset, to start preparing for the winter ahead.

With that being said, I watched this squirrel as he went about the task to bury this prized source of winter food, he had collected. It was funny how the squirrel would dig a little and then pop up his head and look around, as too see if anyone was watching him. He would then look around for a little bit, and then go back to digging the hole for the nut. The squirrel had a nervous likeness about him the whole time he was working on completing this one duty. I wonder what was going through the mind of that animal as he worked on burying that valuable source of winter food. Was he concerned if others were watching him and would know where one of his possessions where hidden? Did he fear for his life while he was out in the open digging the hole for the nut? Is he feeling good about storing up this food for the long winter to feed his family? Maybe all of these and several other things were going through his brain, while working on the project at hand. After a little while he would have the completed job finished, with the nut buried and covered up. The spot he had chosen in the yard was not even noticeable from the hole he had made.

As I was watching this crazy little long tailed animal I was thinking, how does he remember where he buried all of his nuts for the winter storage? Surely he could not remember, where each nut, was. Did God give him an eternal GPS to track the exact location of where each nut was, that he had put underground? I can't even remember where I put my keys yesterday, let alone a whole bunch of nuts. Sometimes we have quite a long winter in Michigan. I later found out from talking to my father-in-law, who is a retired teacher, squirrels find those nuts by smell. That does make sense. Maybe I should make a scented car key so I could find them when I lay them down in the house.

As I stood there drinking my coffee and watching that fury little critter bury a few other nuts for the winter, I began to ponder on how much man and this little squirrel had in common. We both are sometimes worried that someone may find our possessions. We both may be fearful when we are out of our comfort zones. We want to provide for our families. We try to prepare for the tough road ahead in our lives. It seems like our work is never done.

After the hyper looking little fellow had left my field of observation, I started thinking of how can I apply these observations and thoughts to my Christian life of what this little squirrel was doing. Am I more concerned about hiding my possessions that were given to me by the Lord, instead of being willing to share them with ones that are in need? Do I trust in the Lord to protect me, when I am out of my comfort zone and doing His work? Am I taking care of my family, with their physical, mental, and spiritual directives? Sometimes the Lord doesn't need to hit us over the head with a baseball bat to get our attention. He can use the smallest thing like that of a little fury creature He created to bring a full grown man to his knees in fellowship with Him.

6 Downhill Skate

It was during the winter of nineteen sixty nine. We had just gotten out of school for the winter break. It was the first day of our winter break and we were already bored. Of course mom had already figured that out and said that we needed to go outside and shovel the snow from the driveway and the sidewalk. With a reluctant sigh, my brothers and I bundled up and when about the assignment given. It did not take us long to finish it and move back into the house. Of course after a few minutes we were bored again.

Someone had a great idea to see if we could go out and go skating at a local small pond with some of the neighborhood kids. Mom told us to bundle up good and then to be back before dark. After grabbing our skates and on the way to the pond we were able to collect a couple of the neighborhood guys on the way. When we arrive at our destination it seemed that the temperature had dropped quite a bit. That did not deter us from trying to accomplish our mission. When we reached the skating pond there were a few of the other neighborhood guys there. All in total we had amassed about eleven fellows between the ages of ten and twelve. With that many young, bored, and energetic preteens, something was going to happen. It was not a matter of if but when!

After a while of skating and goofing off, someone had the brilliant ideal of the downhill skate competition. By that time it had gotten pretty cool outside on that wintery overcast day. This small pond was located at the bottom of a small hill with a small stream about four feet across and only about two feet in depth. There was about six feet of flat surface between the bottom of the hill and the edge of the stream, with another three feet between it and the pond. It was a perfect launch pad to jump the stream and land on the pond. At the top of the hill to the bottom of it, was only about seventy yards. All eleven of us, huddled together, and started devising a great engineering plan of the 20th century, for this feat, we were embarking on.

At a length of twenty minutes the great mission was set in place and ready to start. Four guys would run home and get some five gallon buckets. Four other guys would run home and get some of those flat plastic sleds, and round saucers. The others would go get some shovels for clearing the snow from the pond. Everyone was to meet back at the pond as soon as possible to start the work on this massive engineering job, and to get things going for the competition.

With time against us to build this engineering marvel, all of us would run like the wind to obtain the tools we needed for the construction process. After a little while the crew had all shown up and the work was beginning to start. Guys were going down the hill to work on flattening out the snow. Others clearing the pond with the shovels of the accumulated snow cover. Some were breaking up the thin cover layer of ice forming on the creek. The guys with the buckets had hauled some water and poured it on the jump and landing areas of the project. After the snow had been packed on the hill from the guys with the sleds and saucers, we started to haul the water to the starting point on the hill, so we could pour it down the slope to freeze. After quite a few trips up and down the hill with the water, it had become very slippery. After a couple of hours and a lot of work the massive task had been completed.

It was now meeting time to set the rules and see would volunteer for the first run. Who would be the first to feel the thrill of victory, or the agony of defeat? The rules where quite simple. Whoever was able to clear the stream and slide the farthest on the pond was the winner. The time now was to see who would be the first to volunteer to make the first jump. Of course no one stepped up right away to take the first plunge. After much silence someone said the magic words, I will go first. We all climbed to the top of the hill, and had accumulated at the launching pad. At that point all of us had laced up our skates, and ready to go.

As we were looking down the hill, the freshly laid water from the stream, was shining very brightly from the cold air freezing it. The young fellow that stepped up in the meeting to go first, started to have second thoughts about doing it, while standing on the launching pad, at the top of the hill. Boys will be boys, and one of the other fellows snuck up behind him and gave him a hefty push, and down he went. As he was going and picking up speed, it was a miracle he was still on his feet. He hit the bottom of the hill and at the jump area he made a perfect jump over the stream landing on the ice cover pond, sliding a long way. The cheers for him could be heard, throughout the small little valley the pond was sitting in. At that point the rest of us could not wait to take our turn. After that some of us fell in the stream getting wet and others fell on the way down the ice covered hill. All in all it was a great way to start the winter vacation from school. Besides it was not about winning any gold medal or prize, but about making that claim, you were the winner of the first ever downhill skate.

In thinking back on this time in my life, how can I apply this to my walk with the Lord Jesus today? Am I building a relationship with Him that will amount to one of the greatest marvels of today's time? Will I be the first one to step up and take the plunge to lead my family unto Him? Am I leaving a type of legacy for Jesus or myself?

7 At The Well

When we were kids we moved around quite a bit. Mostly we would move from the north to the south. The time was about fifty years ago, when I was just going on thirteen years old. We were living in the foothills of the Ozark Mountains. The house we lived in, did not have any running water or an indoor bathroom. The old outhouse is another story. When you needed a bath you had to cart in water from the outside well. Of course when you were thirteen years old a bath was not that important, let alone carrying in a bunch of water to take one. It was not much of a house, but we were happy, at the time. Today that would be considered as totally living off grid. Back then in that part of the country, it was just known as living a normal daily life.

Ok let me get to telling you about the chore of the water well assignment by our parents. Each kid was assigned to have the duty of filling the water barrel once a day. The job consisted of grabbing a couple of buckets with lids and going outside to collect water, from a covered artisan well. The water well was about, forty yards from the house. The distance to carry the water was not too far. The only problem was that electric cow fence the farmer had put up too keep the cows in and other critters out. It seemed like every time I went to go under that fence, I would bump it and get a little charge from it. After a while I started to think of ways to get out of having to fill that water barrel. Pretty soon my parents had caught on and told me to figure out a solution or suffer the alternative. Of course the alternative was much more of a painful thing to deal with then that bite of that electric cattle fence, if you know what I mean.

The battle began with the cattle fence and me. After much thought I went to the local gas station and ask some of the old timers, that hung around there what would be good to prevent that fence from zapping me almost each time I had to fetch water. Of course some of the old timers would come up with their own theory and ideas on how to solve the problem. After much discussion it was agreed to that I would need to use some type of stick to lift the electric wire up higher to get under the fence. Being a big kid, after trying this a few times, I still would feel the sting of the shock once in a while.

Oh well, I had to go back to the drawing board. Then the light bulb came on. I heard one of the older gentlemen say that rubber would shield you from electric shock. After getting permission from my mom, I ran back to the small gas station and asked the owner if I could have an old worn out inner tube, from him. For ones that have never heard of an inner tube, unlike today's tubeless tires, it is like a balloon that went inside a tire to keep it inflated. The owner said sure I could have one, as long as I did not make any slingshots with it. Once again that is another story of the trouble gotten into, with the homemade slingshot, down the road.

After returning home with that dirty old inner tube, the design process of operation Stop That Zap had begun. I had taken a pair of old scissors found in the barn and started to cut a piece of that dirty inner tube to a length of about three feet. I then made a cut length wise along the three foot length of the tube. After that I cut three strips of rubber from the left over inner tube, to be able to tie the three foot piece onto that low hanging wire. After all of the pieces had been cut, it was time to install and test the finished product.

Out to the electric fence I went with the newly created inner tube pieces in hand. While stalling and looking at the wire for a little while then building up the courage to test and see if the rubber would really stop the electric from shocking me, it was time to test out the rubber theory. I took the large piece of rubber and carefully laid it on the fence without touching the wire. I then took my hand and quickly touched the rubber. All had went well. I then proceeded to wrap my hand around the rubber covered wire and was completely protected from the nasty sting of the electricity. After carefully taking the tie strips and securing the large piece of rubber to the wire, the mission had be completed. At last the war with the electric cow fence had been won. The next time I had to tote water, I would be ready to go. Needless to say it was not too long after I entered the house and my mother saw all of the dirt on me from the dirty old inner tube. At that point I had to fetch some water for a bath.

As I think about this and wonder what lessons Jesus has for me from being tortured from that electric cow fence. Was He teaching me to obey my parents when given a directive by them? Sometimes do I need to get down on my knees for direction from Him? Is He teaching me to think outside of the box, to accomplish His work? Or maybe the sweet taste of that hard earned water is just a reminder of the wonderful grace He has for me. I am sure that the Lord will have me ponder and think of another time He has protected and made a way for me, in dealing with the struggles on earth.

8 Train Whistle

I was setting at home one evening and I heard that familiar sound of the whistle of the train going through town. It had triggered a thought of a time when I was a kid and we were living in the small town of Rochelle, Illinois. At that time we lived very close to a switching terminal and a large outside unloading and loading dock for the rail cars. Being a young boy and close to an operation like that, it was an opportunity to get into a whole lot of trouble.

Some of the neighborhood guys would gather at my house and watch to see what would be unloaded from the rail cars, and loaded on to the semi-trucks for transporting, to the final destination for that freight. Sometimes we were able to see the brand new cars that were going to the dealers to sale. Oh how we dreamed of driving a brand new mustang or corvette. Well any way back to reality. Around the dock area were several types of debris, like metal banding, wood pallets and cardboard from the freight being loaded and unloaded. Now the cardboard we would retrieve is a whole other story in itself.

One of the prized pieces of that debris to collect was a piece of that metal banding. The banding was shaped about half inch in width, maybe sixteen of an inch in thickness, with small holes every inch, running the entire length of the metal banding. Now the cool thing we did with that metal banding, was to cut it off at every fourth hole. We then would fold the strap between the second and third hole, so that these holes would line up where one would be on top of the other. Now after bending and getting everything lined up you could put it in your mouth, positioning it just right, you could blow through it and make the loudest whistle sound you ever heard. Of course if it was taken away there was a long supply of banding to make another. Our group of young fellows would have one of these on our person, to use for a code of communication we had developed, among our little group.

One day one of the knuckle head guys pulled his homemade whistle out of his pocket in class at school and put it in his mouth. The nice thing with this whistle, you could hide it completely in your mouth. After much practice a person could control the loudness, pitch, and make all different kinds of sounds with it. While setting in class he would make some different kinds of sounds. All of us other gents knew what was happening. He proceeded to do this for a couple of days, and totally sending the teacher into a different mindset. Well like all things, it is not a matter of if you get caught, but when you get caught. And again Mrs. Smith finally caught up with him. Now back then at school, the price you paid for your ways of error would result into, what some would consider a form of capital punishment today? Now back then you did not even think about going home and telling your parents you got disciplined at school for something you did. The price you had to pay at home was far worse than the price you paid at school. As a young boy you would learn quite quickly of what you could and could not get by with. With my parents it always seemed like I could not get by with anything. At one point I sometimes thought that my mother must have had eyes in the back of her head.

As I remember back on this time, in what way is the Lord having me apply this flashback to my life today. Do I praise Him and thank Him for the price of capital punishment He paid on the cross for me? How much do I communicate with Him? Am I spreading the Good News He has to offer the lost, or just keeping it to myself? Yes like my mom, with those eyes in the back of her head, the Lord does see all that I do in my daily walk with Him!

9 Slingshot Troubles

It was a bright sunny summer day and again we were told to go outside and start the morning chores. Once again it was my time to fill the water barrel. It was a good thing that I made that inner tube cover for the electric cattle fence. After the morning chores were done, mom told us to stay outside and play. She said not to come in until it was lunch time. Now it was time to find something to do.

Should I go to the nearby pond and go swimming or wander in the woods looking for adventure? Now after a twelve year old was forced to make a critical decision, swimming would be fun, but the woods won out. The type of adventure in the woods had to be thought out and a plan put into place. All of a sudden it dawned on me, about what the gas station owner had said, regarding the inner tube. Yes being a twelve year old boy and the thought of going on an adventure in the forest was the only thing to do. With going to the woods, I will need to carry some type of a proper self-defense weapon. The weapon of a slingshot, was a must have item for the adventure. Anyway, that was my excuse to make one. Everybody needs some type of firepower to ward off any critter attacks in the dark dense woods of the Ozark Mountains. The beginning of secret mission impossible for making the sling shot was officially starting.

Now begins the task of making that item of the slingshot. I went to the barn and retrieved the piece of the left over rubber inner tube. After cutting out a couple of long strips about one inch wide and twelve inches in length these would work perfect. I then cut out a pouch for the stone to sit into. I was able to find a small spool of thin rope to attach, the rubber to the wood. The next thing to do, was to search for the perfect piece of wood for attaching the cutout rubber items to. I proceeded to climb one of the old oak trees that were in the yard and behold there was the perfect little dead branch, which had that desirable shape of a Y I needed. Being young, I had not thought of bringing the small hand saw to cut that branch off, so down the tree I went to get the saw. Maybe that is where they came up with the old saying to learn to work smarter and not harder, by making sure you have a plan in place to make it easy on yourself to get the job done.

After getting all of the parts fabricated, I started the assembly of the slingshot. I would take the ends of the rubber strip and attach them to the ends of the Y part of the sling shot. I was able to take the rope and wrap it around the rubber with many strands, and tying it to the wood, to create a strong bond. After that I took the pouch and cut a couple of holes on each side of it. The rubber strips were threaded through the holes and tied securely with a couple of good knots. The slingshot had now been assembled and ready for a trial run. As all good hunters and adventurers do, I had to name the sling shot. After a short amount of time, the decision was made to call her Old Betsy.

Ok the next step was too gather a few stones from the driveway, for the first official test of the sling shot. I was being cautious, and fearful of getting caught by mom with the newly made weapon. As I went behind the barn and out of view from the house, I would constantly look to make sure no one could see me. Not too far from the barn was that old devil of wire for the electric cattle fence. A thought came to my mind, now I had an opportunity of giving that old fence a little punishment back, from it zapping me all those times I had to gather water for the barrel.

The first shot to come out of the slingshot aimed at the fence post was from a distance of about ten yards. I loaded the stone in the pouch, pulled the sling shot back, away the stone flew and missed the fence post. One thing I did learn, was that the slingshot, held together and did not break apart. Being determined to inflict some pain on the fence I loaded up the slingshot and moved closer toward the fence for the second shot.

After releasing the pouch with the stone from the grip of my fingers, it flew with a mighty force toward the fence post. It hit the post and bounced back at me. I was not quick enough to dodge out of its path toward me. With the stone ricocheting off of the fence post, it had hit me just below my right eye. Now that the blood was streaming down my face I had no choice, but to go in and seek mom's help. The first thing I did was to hide the slingshot in the barn before going in the house.

As I walked into the house mom noticed right away that blood was running down my face. She said, go into the kitchen and take off your shirt. After a while when mom cleaned me up and said it looked like I did not need stiches, she asked the dreaded question I did not want to answer for. Yes the question was, what and how did the injury happen to me. As I have learned in the past, that the truth was the best way to go, instead of a lie. The price you paid for a lie was higher than when you told the truth. When it was all done I wound up having to turn over the slingshot and the adventure into the woods never happened that day. Well, it wasn't the adventure I had planned.

When thinking back on this one little event in my life, I think of how Jesus was looking over me. Did that stone fly back and hit me in the face so that I would be unable to go on that adventure into the woods, and possibly run across a bear, or mountain lion? Was I being disciplined by making the slingshot, when I was not supposed to? Did the Lord remind me that vengeance is His by shooting at the fence post? Being a Christian I will someday have the chance to ask Him these questions.

10 Pig Bust 'in

It was in the year of nineteen sixty eight, and being about twelve years old, at the peak of rodeo season. We were living in the boot heel of Missouri. At that time we lived in a rural area just outside of a town called Popular Bluff. Now in that area going to the local county fair was a big deal. When you were at that age it was a place where you could go and see all kinds of different things. There was also the carnival rides, food trucks and different types of farm items in exhibits. Also it was the biggest rodeo show of the year that Saturday night.

It was early Saturday morning, and time for Uncle Herman to come by and pick us up to go to the county fair. If we went with Uncle Herman, we could get in free, because it was rodeo day and he always entered in one of the competitions, of the rodeo. Mom gave us a couple of dollars each that had been earned from doing some extra chores around the house. We loaded up with Uncle Herman and took off for the fair. There was no allowance given to us kids back then, I think mom just said that, to make us feel like we earned something doing a job. Then again you did not want to receive pay for not doing what you were told, it definitely was not green and white and made out of paper.

The ten minute ride in the back of his old pickup pulling the big horse trailer, was a far cry from a smooth ride in a new big Oldsmobile. Back then the only seat belts we had, were shut up, sit down and hold on. Believe me riding in the back of that old truck and those bumpy roads, you had to hold on for sure. Finally we had arrived at the fairgrounds. We had to help Uncle Herman unload the horses and some of the hay before we were turned loose to discover the sites of the county fair. Uncle Herman told us to meet back at the truck and trailer at a certain time for the ride back home. With our Uncle Herman you had better not be late, or it would be a long walk home that night. After the rodeo was over we met back at the truck for the ride home. Once we had gotten home it was bath and bed time. After being out in the sun at the fair all day, we slept well that night.

I bet you are wondering where the pig bust 'in comes in? Well it started the next day. My brothers and I were bored and needed something to do, while we had been shooed outside from mom. Now boys will be boys. One of us had the bright ideal to head down to the farmers, field of pigs next door and try to see if we could do some pig bust 'in, like we seen the cowboy riders do at the rodeo last night, with the bulls and horses. We then retrieved a piece of rope from the barn and headed down the road. After crossing over the farmer's fence and into the field with the pigs, the first order of business, was to lasso one of the pigs and see who was going to ride it first. After all was decided the youngest brother, would go first.

We lassoed one of the pigs that were grazing next to one of the mud holes. Once we got him settled down, Danny climbed aboard and away the pig went. That pig was running and shaking, trying to get him off. The pig hit the mud hole at a speed that was unbelievable. You would think that pigs couldn't ever run fast. When this pig hit the mud hole Danny came flying off that pig with the rope in hand. Needless to say all of the rest of us busted out laughing so hard we could hardly stand up.

You have probably heard the old saying, all is fun and games until someone gets hurt. After a few hours and all of us covered in mud and dirt, no one got hurt but the farmer had shown up to see what was causing all of the noise the pigs were making. Maybe we should change that to all is fun and games until you get caught. The farmer all made us get in the back of his pickup and delivered us back home. Now mom had seen him pull up and she met him at the driveway. At that time we were instructed by mom to go behind the house, hose off and wait there until she came to get us. Mom had talked with the farmer, about us trying to be the first ever pig busters in that county. Shortly after that mom had gotten us some dry clothes, told us to change and head directly to our bedrooms. Yes we heard those dreaded words, stay in your rooms until your father gets home. After dad got home and we paid the price for pig bust 'in that was the last time this fellow ever try to ride a pig. I didn't even want a ham sandwich for a while after that.

Some of the valuable things that I learned through this time and day in my life was, pigs are fast. Just kidding. The price for trying to be a renowned pig buster, is a little more that I am willing to pay. Sometimes we need to look for honest and creative ways to spend our time. When we do something to help others, like extra work around the house, the Lord will reward us. Again Jesus kept one of us from being hurt, from a two hundred pound pig, even when doing something we should not have done.

11 Cardboard Slides

It was around the same time era as when we lived in Illinois for a while. This was when we lived right next to the rail cars loading docks. There sometimes would be large pieces of cardboard from the product that was being loaded or unloaded on the rail cars. Sometimes a group of us boys would snatch up some of this cardboard for the races we were about to have. The guy that ran the loading dock did not mind if we took the large sheets of cardboard. By us taking it away it was less work for him to have to do, in picking it up. I guess you could say that we were recycling that cardboard, in a way. You know when you get a half dozen of twelve or thirteen year old boys together, trouble is brewing.

Now to the most important part of the story. There would be about six of us toting, these large flat pieces, of brown cardboard down the street to the nearby park. In the park was a large grassy covered hill which we used for the cardboard races. At the bottom of the hill was the entry way to the park, with a good size flat area, before the start of the bottom of the hill. On the top of the hill was a large flat area that was perfect for using as the launching area. After reaching the top of the hill, it was once again time to establish the rules for the downhill races of the summer cardboard slides. Not only did we set the rules of the single man competition but we also set the rules of the two man competition.

On that hot summer day, the grass on the hill side had been burn up from the summer sun. Thankfully the grass had been cut short, before being toasted by the summer sun. These were idea conditions for fast speeds down the hill that summer. The rules were quite simple, you could not cross the take off line on your feet and the one that went the farthest, would win that heat. After all heat winners where decided, you would then, have the semifinals until the others had loss and the two final teams were left to race for the win. Now with boys you had to do the best two out of three. There were never any ties in our competitions. We must have winners to receive the traveling homemade trophies, made out of cardboard, in both the single and the two man race. In winter time on that hill, we would have the downhill races, in the snow, but that it another story.

Ok it was time to have the first race. A couple of guys lined up well behind the starting line to get a good running start. The flag was dropped and away they went. Both had a great start and when they came to the line flying in the air and landing, stomach first on their pieces of cardboard, down the hill they went. The speed us incredibly fast, due to the dry grass conditions. Jim was cruising at a great speed, well ahead of Bobby. All of a sudden Jim lost control and flew off of his piece of cardboard, eliminating him from the first singles race of the day. The rest of us, including Jim let out a loud stomach twisting laugh, which could probably be heard all throughout the small park. After a while the singles and the team competitions were decided.

Now when you are a young fellow it does not take you long to get bored with something like cardboard slides, so one of the gang had a great idea. Well it seemed like a great idea at the time. Ok the one who thought of it had to go first. That was the rules of the cardboard slide races. Mister wise guy, we will call him Benny, suggested we ride that cardboard downhill standing up, instead of laying on our stomach. Again being a stupid thing to do, we were all in. Benny took his cardboard and put it at the starting line. He then backed up and took off on a dead run toward the cardboard. When he approached the sheet of cardboard he leaped in the center and down the hill he went. He was able to out distance, any attempt anybody had achieved that day, by sliding all the way to the park entrance. Now all of the rest of us had to have a turn going down that hill standing up. There were times when one of us would fall and a roar of laughter when out. When it was time to go and our sheets of cardboard had worn out, the call for a new kind of trophy and a new name of hillside surfing, was decided on.

When I think back of this time today, my mind wanders what the Lord is having me learn. Is He teaching me that sometimes, teamwork is needed to accomplish the goals He has set for me? Do I need to get out of the way and let Him, or someone else lead? Do I need to make the best and be creative of what I have and what He has given me? He will protect me even when I do some crazy things at times. All in all I am glad, that Jesus is on my side today.

12 Cannon Shot

There was a time when we heard the shot that when around the world. Believe it or not it was not that long ago for a young pup of myself. It all happened in the rural area of Battlecreek, Michigan. Yes that famed city of Tony the Tiger cereal. It was about the year of nineteen sixty eight. My parents decided to visit one of my aunts and her family. Now when you got all of us cousins together, to the sum of five boys, and one girl, there was bound to be trouble or danger in some way.

It was a Saturday afternoon and we just got back to the house from swimming at the local lake, mom and Aunt Billie, had made us lunch. Billie is definitely a name for a girl from the south in the delta area of our country. Of course you know how hungry you can get from a few hours of swimming in the lake. All of us boys were in those teenage years where we could scarf down the groceries. When the lunch time had ended and a couple of us got in trouble at the table with our mothers, we were sent outside, for the rest of the day. In a short period of time after being sent out, we all were getting bored. Five teenage boys, being bored is a very dangerous combination. Cousin Ricky Dale, another southern way to name a child, had the bright idea of building a cannon. So now comes in the danger factor.

We started the project of building the cannon. Someone gathered five empty soda cans and another one retrieved the can opener from the kitchen. How Danny got that can opener past mom and my aunt I will never know. Junior was able to find some strong tape and a nail from the barn. Ronald had hunted up an old tennis ball they used to play stickball with. I was able to find the lawn mower gas can, being the danger factor of the cannon. To build this cannon we would cut the top and bottom of four of the soda cans out. Back then the soda cans were made a little different and stronger than they are today. We took the four cans, without the bottoms and tops, and taped them together. The tape had to be wound around the top and bottom of each can where they met, by stacking one on top of the other and wrapping several times making a good seal. After all four had been connected, it was time to tape the unopened can to the bottom, with the top of it taped to the opened bottom of the cans, stacked on top. After all five cans had been securely attached, we then took the nail and made small hole in the bottom sidewall of the unopened can. At that point the cannon had been assembled and ready to fire.

It had come time to fire the cannon. Who would be the test dummy to do it? After much discussion it was decided that Ricky Dale would be the one, seeing it was his idea, and a friend at school told him how to make it. He proceeded to pour about a bottle cap full of gasoline into the small nail hole. After filling it with the gasoline Ricky Dale then took the cannon and shook it up. The tennis ball was put inside the top opening of the cannon. The cannon was then laid on the makeshift launching stone, pointing toward the barn in the driveway. Ricky Dale then struck a match and held it to the opening in the bottom of the cannon. In an instance, with a loud bang, the cannon had fired and away the tennis ball flew, hitting the large barn door. It was a good thing that the tennis ball was somewhat soft and the door well made. Within a millisecond after the cannon was shot we heard those dreaded words, "boys what are you doing". We had been busted by our mothers. We were caught, red handed in the act. Unfortunately we also heard those other dreaded words, give it to me and wait in your bedrooms until your fathers get home. You would think that one of us geniuses would of thought that the cannon would make a loud enough noise that our mothers would of heard it and we needed to get as far from the house as we could. Then again boys will not sometimes think things through. At that point it was the end of the cannon making times in our lives. We did live to tell our friends about that shot we heard that went around the world.

By the way at this time all of our cousins have passed away, along with my brother. As I smile and think about this time spent with other family members, I still get a smile on my face. We did do some crazy things when we were kids, but we were close and always had fun. Sometimes the Lord will have us see the good in things, even though there is a price to be paid at the time. Does Jesus protect you, from the dangers of others and even from yourself? Have you had that quality time with the Lord and your family? Have you asked Christ into your heart, and heard that shot of Him, that has went around the world, of the price He paid on the cross for you?

13 Lake Swim

My wife and I were at the annual church picnic, being held at a local park, next to the St. Joseph River in Benton Harbor, MI. Setting near the river and looking at the water, a thought came to my mind, when it was the summer of nineteen sixty five. At that time we lived on Little Paw Paw Lake, outside of Coloma, MI. Now this lake was only about a mile across, from one side to other. With it being very shallow near the shores. Mom had given us fifty cents apiece, and told us to get out of the house and take a walk to the store. Now back then fifty cents could be stretched quite far. We would be able to get some candy, a soda, and still have something left over. We could even get that pea shooter, or a small slingshot, but that is another story.

My younger brother Daniel and I decided to swim across the small lake and go to a small convenience store, directly across the lake from where we were living. Besides they say the shortest distance between two points is a straight line, and we wanted to measure that in time with swimming, versus walking extra distance, around the lake. We were a little pass the middle of the lake. Like most of them this was the deepest part. Now as we were swimming along everything was going find and then I heard my brother scream my name about five yards behind me. I then turned around and saw him struggling to keep his head above the water and I immediately swam toward him. As he was going under the water I grabbed him by his hair and lifted him back up. He had taken in some water, and then made a loud coughing sound to spit it out. He was crying and said he was not going to be able to make it to the shore.

Although with no formal training, it was time for me to go into lifeguard mode. After holding him up and treading water for a couple of minutes, I told Daniel to hold onto my shoulder and we would get to the shore. In the process of swimming toward the shore with him holding on to my shoulder, I was beginning to feel the fatigue of all that was happening. Thoughts were going through my mind. Will we make it? Will both of us drown in the lake? How much farther is it to shore? Are the shallows close? After swimming a little more we were getting closer to the shore, I

34

then told my brother we had to stop, because I needed a breather. After treading water for a couple of minutes and looking after him I made the choice of going on. This was do or die time. With my younger brother in tow, and my eye on the convenience store, I mustered up the last of my strength to my arms and legs to try and make it. After what seemed like an eternity my foot touched the bottom of the lake. Finally I had made it to the shallows. We stopped and I told my brother to put his feet down because we had made it.

Both of us walked to the shore and sit down. It took a little while for Daniel and me to get ourselves together and go inside the store. After catching my breath I asked Danny what happened. He said that his legs were hurting him and he could not hardly move them. We both agreed not to say anything to mom. With brothers and parents, it has always been an unwritten rule not to mention things like this to one of our parents. I wonder what my children have not told me regarding various events in their lives.

While this time back in the day was running through my small brain I started thinking what our Savior Jesus Christ was telling me. Could it be that we are truly our brother's keeper? Am I giving all I have to reach the goals of His work for me? Do I have my eyes on Him, and am I focused on the prize He has for me? Am I putting material things like that pea shooter before Him? When we are remembering of those times back in the day, let us praise the Lord our God for the many blessings we have received!

14 Wintertime Sheeting

It was the winter of nineteen sixty three. In my opinion it was a good time in history for the United States, or was I too young and naïve to know any better. I think back to a quote that John F Kennedy had in one of his speeches which belonged to Herbert Hoover about "Two Chickens in Every Pot". Well anyway it seemed like good times back in that time of my life.

Ok I bet all of you are wondering what wintertime sheeting is. Some would call it crazy, some would call it stupid and dangerous. And if you were young and dumb, like I was at that time you might even call it fun. To do the wintertime sheeting, the conditions had to be perfect. Back in those days during a Michigan winter they did not use a lot of salt or sand on the roads. If you lived in the city or the heights like we did, you just learned how to drive even if there was a build of ice or snow on the roads. Most of the small towns just did not have the tax revenue to be able to take care of the slick roads like they do now days. Ok the only rule in wintertime sheeting is <u>Don't Get Caught.</u>

On a cold dark evening, usually there would be a group of us hanging out down town, looking for something to do. If the evening was cold and the roads where iced over we would look for a car moving at somewhat of a slow speed where we could run and catch it. Now when that car was spotted we would take off at a quick running pace to try to catch up to it. Yes you probably guessed what wintertime sheeting is by now. We would catch up with the car and grab onto the back bumper, hold on and go for a ride. While holding onto the bumper there are a few things you needed to do to stay alive. These things were number one, keep at a low squat, as to not be seen by the driver or passengers. Number two be at one of the corners in the back so that you could keep an eye on what was ahead. Number three, be on constant alert of what was behind you at all times. Number four, always keep a lookout for your getaway avenue. And number five, probably the most important thing always and I mean always be on the lookout for a dry spot in the road, which may throw you for a severe case of road rash. One thing about doing the wintertime sheeting, was when you went home and settled into the bed, you slept very well that night from being tired and cold.

All was going well with the wintertime sheeting that year until one of the fellows in the group got caught. We will call the young guy Tommy Smith. The funny part of it was that it was his own father that caught him. It had happened that Tommy and one of the other guys had spotted this 1957 Chevy coming down the road. Tommy said, that looks like my dad's car. As knuckle head boys will do, one of us said are you chicken? Tommy said no way. Then one of the fellows said prove it, and the dare was now on. Tommy and James took off on a run toward the car. First one to latch on was James, and he took the passenger's side of the rear bumper. Tommy then took the driver's side. As the rest of us were watching the car must have went only about thirty yards down the slick covered road and all of a sudden we seen Tommy take a tumble and the brake lights came on the Chevy. The thought of, Tommy must of hit a dry spot went through our minds. As we were watching Mr. Smith had stopped the car and then jumped out of his door. By that time James had let go and taken off down one of the side streets running with all he had. Tommy was still on the ground. The rest of us had also taken off running to our homes.

The next day we saw Tommy at school, and he was walking using a crutch. Tommy had said that he hit a dry spot and that's what knocked him off of the bumper. He was taken to the emergency room by his parents. He had a sprung ankle and a small case of road rash. All in all he survived the spill very well. Tommy was grounded for the next month and told by his parents that the police and the rest of our parents would be told of what we were doing. At that point the wintertime sheeting actives had come to an end.

Now that I think back as a parent myself, I think of how stupid and dangerous of a thing it was to do. Possibly one of the problems was we did not have any thing at that time to keep us young men out of trouble. I also now think of how the Lord has a message in all of this to me. Going through life and being a Christian today, there will be dry spots that I will have to deal with in my life. Will I be able to dodge that dry spot? Will I go to Him and be able to land on my feet when that dry spot is in front of me? Will I look into His word for what He has for me to make my future a smooth ride? With His help I am able to ignore any peer pressures and do the right and faithful things in my life. Praise to the Lord that He has always watched over me and is still looking out for me.

15 Fruit Market Summer

It was the start of summer time and school was going to be out in a couple of weeks. I had been thinking this was going to one of the greatest summer ever. We had not planned on going down south to spend the summer with, my grandparents. I would be able to hang out with my friends all that summer. I could not hardly wait for school to be out. My friends and I were already making plans of our activities for the summer. I was looking forward to the trip to see my first major baseball game at the Chicago Cubs, Wrigley field. What happened at the ball game trip is another story, of a learned lesson.

We were living in the heights and the walk home from school was a little over a half mile. Each day as I walked in front of the major fruit market, where all of the local produce and fruits would come, to be sold, there was a lot of activity going on. There would be semi-trucks coming and going all in the day time, hauling fresh fruits and vegetables to various parts of the United States. This was a very busy place that time of the year, as early harvest items were coming and going. Not only did they do the local farmers, but they also would receive items from other parts of the country, that were ready for sale. There was always something going on there during that time of the year. Every once in a while we could get one of the semi-drivers to sound the air horn on their trucks.

One day while walking home from school, going in front of the market, a man shouted out to me, hey you come here. I went over to where he was and a few other guys that were unloading watermelons, which had come up from down south. Being a big kid that I was at the age of thirteen, he asked if I would be interested in making a few dollars. I said of course and asked him what he needed me to do. The gentleman wanted me to help finish the unloading of the watermelons. After about a couple of hours we had completed the job and he paid, me with a ten dollar bill. He also told be to stop by after school tomorrow and he would have more work for me to do. I did let the boss man know that I would ask my mother if it was ok, and let him know tomorrow. Now back then, a ten dollar bill to a thirteen year old was a big deal to have. I was thinking if I could work until school was out, I would have some money for the summer, how great would that be!

Ok it was time to high tail it home. I was already forty five minutes past the time to check in with my mother after school. After I had made it home, my mother asked where I have been. After all these years, and as I have seen, I think that all mothers are born with that ability to give you the look. You know that look that is basically saying you messed up and now, can almost be considered a dead man walking. After I had told my mom about the opportunity to make a few dollars, that day, the pressure of facing the gallows was over. I also asked her if I could work for the guy after school again tomorrow. She said that was fine but make sure that I told him I had to be home by six p.m., and to get his phone number. Also I was to make sure that I gave him our phone number. After our conversation was done and I dodged the bullet, I was told to do my homework, then get a bath. Soon after that it was dinner time, at the table. Unlike today that is one thing that my parents insisted on was we had to be at the table for dinnertime. Not only did you get that look from mom, but if you were not at the table, you missed dinner. After going to bed that night and moving those twenty pound water melons, I slept like a log.

The next day school was out and I headed straight to the fruit market. After finding Mr. Johns and exchanging information, of time to be home, phone numbers, etc. he put me to work. This time we were loading strawberry crates onto a semi-trailer. This was a refrigerated trailer with the air starting to cool it down as we were loading the berries. Up front near the cooling unit was cooler than the rear, of the trailer. There were two men up front and a line of about four others passing the crates of berries to the two stackers. When you stacked strawberries in a semi there is a special way to do it, using wooden slats to lock them together. After proper stacking of berries, there would be good ventilation all the way around each crate to prevent rotting. Suddenly someone said it was break time and to take fifteen. There were about three guys that jumped down off the loading dock and pulled out a couple of dice. It must have been pay day for them. One of the guys asked if I had any money and wanted to shoot craps with them. I said no and started to watch. After a while and the money was flying the time had come to go back to work. The workers picked up their cash and we all went back to work. I guess that was the summer I learned the game of craps. After a couple of hours we were done and it was time, for me to go home. Mr. Johns paid me and said see you tomorrow at the same time, away I went, happy as a lark.

As I was walking into the back door I heard my mom on the phone and the name Mr. Johns. When my mother had hung up the phone, she said that was Mr. Johns, asking if, I could work for him all this summer. My mom had told Mr. Johns that I could and that he could give me the details the next day I seen him. As you have now figured out my greatest summer ever was not going to happen, because I would be working for Mr. Johns. For a thirteen year old the good thing about this, is that I would have some cash in my pocket.

As I think about this today, what is the Lord, having me learn and be able to pass onto my children? Does He want me to teach, that sometimes we are not going to have that greatest summer of our lives? Hard work will build character in a person. Our plans may not be the same as God's plan? Am I willing to gamble like shooting craps, and go through life without Jesus? Yes I believe that all mothers, have been blessed with the look.

16 Cruise 'in The Plaza

The year was nineteen sixty nine. I had worked and saved my money all summer. As a teenager I had received my official driver's license. The summer was over and I had just bought that 1961 Buick, my first car. It was somewhat of a beater and I only paid seventy five dollars for it. The car did burn a little oil, but that was better than walking or riding a bicycle when you are sixteen. Of course I had to do a little work and spend a couple of dollars to make it road worthy. After all was done, dad gave me the approval to put it on the road. I called my buddy Rod and asked if he wanted to go cruising with me. Rod did not hesitant to say yes and I told him what time I would pick him up. After picking Rod up it was now time to go cruise 'in at the plaza.

In the town that we lived in there was somewhat of a large plaza. We had the Five and Dime store, Walgreen's with the soda fountain, Movie House and Henry's Burger Drive Inn with lots of other small stores and shops. Back then we could get Henry's hamburgers ten for a dollar. Oh and there was the department store called Goldblatts. This was a place that I worked at one time, but that is another story.

It was a Friday night and everyone would be at the plaza. The plaza was setup so that there was a parking lot in the middle and all of the stores were on the outside of the lot. The lot was about a half mile long and a half mile in width, with the driving area set up on the outside. With the lot and shops being setup this way, you could drive completely around and park in front of every store there. On Friday night it seemed that all of the local gearheads were there circling around the plaza looking for a drag race. Personally my car was not set up to drag race, but it was cool just to be able to drive around that circle and burn up some gasoline. I remind my wife every once in a while that, back then I could fill the tank, take her out for a burger and a movie, for less than ten dollars. Most of the cars would have their windows down with the music going. You definitely could tell which of the cars had the new eight tracks, with the big speakers. Yes then the eight track players were the hot ticket item for your car. Every once in a while some hot rod would do a short burn out and fill the air with tire smoke. Of course every so often the police would have a guy pulled over making out a ticket for him.

It seemed like almost every Friday night there would be a drag race. All of a sudden there would be signs that a race was coming. As you cruised there would be a few cars parked with their hoods up. Two guys would give a girl some money for her to hold. The bunch of cars that were parked, with the hoods up would start to leave at a fast pace. At that point it was race time. In a matter of a few minutes the parking lot would clear out. Everyone knew where the secluded race spots were at, so all of us headed there. If you were not sure you just would follow the pack. Just make sure if you were some of the last few leaving and the police was following you, make sure you went somewhere else. This was one of the unwritten codes of cruising the plaza.

We had just arrived at the straight flat pavement where the drag race was to begin. After parking and getting out to watch the race, my buddy and I sat on top of the hood. Back then when we set on top of the hood, there was no worry about putting a dent in it like what would happen to today's cars. As we were watching all of a sudden out of nowhere there were red and blue lights flashing everywhere. The police were coming down the road. Every car there had started up and was fleeing the scene. My budding and I took off in a completely different direction of all of the others. My heart was pumping, all I could think about was I am going to get a ticket on the first day of driving my car I just got on the road? Am I going to jail? Will I lose my driving rights forever? Is mom and dad going to kill me? What is going to happen?

At that point I told my buddy that we had better head home. Rod only lived a couple of blocks from me, so I dropped him off. As I was heading home it seemed like it was taking an eternity to get to my house. As I walked in the house mom said, "You are home early well before your curfew". All I said back was, "Yes it just seemed a little boring, so I thought I would come home early due to having to work in the morning".

Looking back at this evening in my young life I think about what the Lord is telling me. Do we sometimes think that we are not

43

breaking the rules, even though we are not the ones drag racing? Can all of our dreams be taken away in a flash? Do we choose our friends with His direction? Do we know with Jesus, we may be able to run, but we will never be able to hide? The choice is ours.

17 Pea Shooters In The House

It happened one of those summers we went to spend with the grandparents in the south flat lands of Arkansas. This was part of the delta country of the United States. Yes it would be a hot summer compared to the summers in the southwest area of Michigan. There would be no breeze coming off of Lake Michigan. Then again when you are a kid the heat seemed like it did not bother you. That summer was when some of our cousins from the Holland Michigan area would be down there also. Our grandparents would have a house full of five rowdy boys for about six weeks. My grandparents truly loved their grandchildren. They were fair but firm. They lived in a large house, which was capable of holding all of us. Our grandfather loved to have us down for the summer. This was a chance to put all of us to work. He would have many chores for us to do. As most southern families they had a big garden, and down south you could get two complete gardens a summer. Grandmother would home can items from the garden all summer, so she always had something for us to do. Now the home canning is another story.

The day after our parents had dropped us off, Grand, as we called him, made a deal with all of us boys. He said that as long as we worked hard, he would give us a dollar at the end of the week. He then said we could go to the five and dime store in town to spend our money. Back then a dollar to a ten year old was a lot of money. Grand would usually wake us up early in the morning and assign those daily work duties to each of us. I can remember what he would say when he came into the bedrooms to get us up, time to get up and get with it, day light is a burning. In the beginning I would mumble about having to get up early. After I thought about it, Grand was looking out after us, by getting the work done, before the heat of the day.

We had finished our first week of work, and it was pay day. Grand had given all of us a dollar apiece. We were on our way to town to spend that precious dollar bill. After a while one of us spotted the ultimate thing to spend some of our money on. Yes it was the prized pea shooter package. For those of you that do not know what a pea shooter is, it is quite simple. The package consisted of a small cloth bag of dried hard peas, and an oversized straw that the peas would fit in. As you probably have figured out by now, all you had to do was, put the pea in your mouth and shoot it through the straw, like a blowgun with a dart. Of course each one of us boys had to get the pea shooter package for only twenty five cents. As with rowdy boys the main thing was not to get caught. After buying the pea shooter package, penny candy, sodas, it was time to head back to the grandparents' house.

On the way home in the back of Grands pickup truck we all talked about have a shooting contest with the pea shooters. We could not hardly wait to get home. Once we pulled into the driveway and jumped out of the back of the truck we headed to the woods behind the barn. Grand was on his way into the house for that afternoon nap he always took. After a couple of hours the contest was over and some of us had run out of peas. With Grands big garden one of us thought of the dried peas in the barn for the next seasons planting. We all thought great now we had a big supply of dried peas, as long as we did not get caught.

It was Sunday morning and like we did every Sunday, it was time to get ready for church. I heard my grandmother say, "I wonder where all of these dried peas came from". She then proceeded to take a broom and sweep them up. Remember boys will be boys. We had started shooting each other in the house with the pea shooters. After we came home from church and were changing into our play clothes before lunch, some of us were goofing around and shooting each other with peas. Grand came in the room to tell us to go down for lunch and busted all of us in the act. The fatal words came out of Grand's mouth, "Round all of the pea shooters up and give them to me". Shortly after that we heard him telling our grandmother of what we were doing. Punishment time was coming. While we were at the table our grandmother made the statement that Grand had given her the shooters and it was her decision to administer the punishment. She said "the shooters will be put in her china cabinet at a level for us to see and we would never get them back". After dinner we all had to sweep and mop the floors in the whole house to make sure we cleaned up any leftover peas. The rest of the summer every time we walked by the chia cabinet and saw those pea shooters we were reminded of the trouble that all of us had gotten into.

Being very close to sixty years old, my wife and I were visiting relatives down south that lived in the same town of my grandparents. We were at one of my aunt's house, when she came out of her kitchen with a pea shooter. She said it was mine from my grandmother's china cabinet and asked if I wanted it back. When I saw it, I could not hardly believe it. I had a flash back of that time when we were all around the dinner table, receiving our judgement and hearing my grandmother telling us what the punishment would be. I told my aunt to keep it, because our grandmother said they now belonged to her and we would not get them back.

As I relate this to my Christian way of life today, I think of what the Lord is telling me. God teaches us that we are loved by Him, even when we get into trouble. The Lord is right beside us through our times of punishment. One thing to remember, when breaking the rules, it is not if you get caught, but when you get caught. Also when we are offered something that we know we are not supposed to receive it, be of integrity and honor our elders.

18 Goldblatts Gold

As I was thinking back to the time when I was around fifteen years old I had just received my workers permit in the mail. If some of you remember back then if you were a minor you had to have that permit to be able to be employed by several types of businesses. With this permit the company you worked for had to follow certain rules set in place by the government. There was also designated hours that a minor could only work. Along with this program, the schools had a program called Co-Op that would work with local businesses to introduce the students to the world of getting, holding, and building a relationship with various companies in the community. Co-Op was another story. I am not sure if the schools still do the Co-Op program now days. I do firmly believe that it is a great program to have in the schools to help young people mature and learn to be a strong working member of the community.

A couple of days after I received my permit I started working for the Goldblatts department store. Back in the day, Goldblatts was a type of store like the modern Kohl's, Sears, and JC Penny's is today. Being a big kid, I was able to get a job in the furniture and carpet department. Back then was the time that carpet for the floors was more popular than hard wood floors and tile. The duties of my job were to help move and load furniture and carpets for the customers and cleaning the show room areas along with any other thing the boss told me to do. One of my favorite things to do was to cut a piece of carpet and help load it up for the customer. We had a machine that would lift the roll of carpet off of the floor. After that you would roll out and measure a piece for the required length. After all measurements were double checked you then would take a long piece of pipe that had a channel cut out the length of the pipe and match it up with the premeasured marks on the carpet. After that you would insert a tool that had a razor blade and long rope attached to it. When you pulled the tool through the cut out in the channeled pipe, it would cut the carpet at the needed length. After that we would roll the carpet up and load it onto the customer vehicle. I always enjoyed the part of talking with the customer and hearing about their remolding projects. Back then customer service was a big part in making a sale to people. Speaking of customer service I am reminded of the time when I was a gas jockey, but that is another story.

I had completed my first week of work at the Glodblatts store and it was pay day. It was time to go home and I had asked my boss if I would be receiving a check from him. The boss had told me that he would give me a slip and I would need to take it to the pay master to collect my wages for the week. The paymaster's office was right next to the time clock where we had to punch in and out when being on the job. When I went to the paymaster window which was a little window next to the time clock that had some steel bars and a small shelf on it, there were a couple of other employees in line, ahead of me. I had often wondered what that window with the bars was for. After waiting a couple of minutes in line it was my turn to step up and get the pot of gold at the end of the work rainbow. All week I was thinking what was I going to do with all of the big money I received that payday.

I gave the lady at the window the slip of paper my boss had given me. She said that she had to look and make sure that the hours my boss had on the slip matched up with the punches on my time card. After a couple of minutes she gave me a little gold colored envelope about three inches by two inches. She told me to open it and take a look to make sure it was correct. I think that she was helping me, knowing that it was my first pay day there. After looking inside the envelope there was no check, just cash and a piece of paper. I smiled and thought great cash, no checks to have to deal with. After counting it, I mentioned to her that I thought that my pay was a little short. As she smiled back at me, she said ok, take out your check stub and let's go over it together. Little did I know, I was about to learn a work life lesson right there. I think she knew that I did not realize that there would be taxes deducted from my pay each period. After learning that the government had to get there part of my pay each week the amount of money I thought I was going to make changed. After the paymaster explained all of the deductions taken out of my pay she just smiled and said welcome to the working world. That pot of Gold was now not as big as I first thought.

As a Christian I think back to this time in my life and the lessons I have learned the world seems to be a place of take, were the Lord is one of giving. Our God does want to give us all of our desires and wants. Sometimes for our on good, He will protect us by not giving us what we think we need or want. The question I have for myself and others is, do we want to be the type of Christian that would rather take than give? As always we have a choice in the way we want to be.

19 Swinging For The Fence

It was the summer of 1960, and I was just thirteen years old. Our team's baseball coach had planned a trip for the team to go to a Chicago Cubs baseball game at Wrigley Field in Chicago, Illinois. I remember it like it was just yesterday. The weather was perfect, and the stands were filled with baseball fans. The bus ride seemed like it took forever to get to the field. Once we got there the line was a little long and the wait seemed like it took quite a while to get pass the gate. After what seemed like an eternity we finally made it to our seats. The grass on the field was a beautiful green the dirt in the infield between the bases was clean and looked almost like the sand on a tropical beach. The bases were a pure snow like white, just asking to be stepped on. Being the first baseman on the little league team I was glad we had seats near the first base area. The field and the stadium gave me the feel of a magical place.

The game was going great and the Cubs were winning. One of my team mates asked if I wanted to go with him to get a coke or something to eat at the concession stand. I said sure why not. After we had made the trip up the stairs and to the concession stand the line there was quite long. I was very limited on the money that I had to spend, so I ordered myself a small soda. I wanted to make sure that I had some money to spend on a souvenir to take home. I had been saving the money for a while from doing some odd jobs like mowing and raking yards of people in the neighborhood. Soon we made our way back to our seats to finish watching the ball game.

It was the start of the seventh inning and our coach told all of us if we wanted to buy any souvenirs, go to the bathroom, or the concession stand, now was the time. We would be heading straight to the bus as soon as the game was over. I was thinking great now is the time to go get an item to take home to remember the time I went to the game. One of my team mates and I then headed to the souvenir shop to pick up something to take home. While we were in the shop I went to pull my wallet out to check if I had enough money to pay for an item that I wanted. Much to my surprise my wallet was gone. I then told my team member that I had to go back to my seat for something and I would see him back with the group. I then ran back to where I was sitting to watch the game and looked all around the area to see if my wallet had fell out of my pocket. After a little while I came to the conclusion that my wallet and money was gone. Did someone pick my pocket at the game with all of the people shuffling around? Did my wallet fall out while I was going up and down the stairs? I guess I will never know what happened that day.

After being broke, hungry, tired, and heart broken, the ride home from the game was a long one. Although after all that happened I did have fun for most of the trip hanging out with the guys. As I think about this experience and now being a born again believer, I see how the Lord was teaching and preparing me for the future. I learned that money is not everything and we will not get all we want in this life. Friendships are more valuable than any amount of money we have. The Lord is our best friend and He will be at our side through all disappointments which come our way. He is setting right next to us on that long ride home.

20 Six Men Bobsled

It was the winter of 1961, and we were visiting my aunt and uncle in Holland, Michigan. I always loved to go to their house and hang out with my four cousins. We were all around the same age. Now when the six of us got together there was bound to be some mischief that was going to happen. They lived in the middle of town in a big three story house. Of course there would be a lot of neighborhood kids that would get together and have a stickball game, hide and seek, or some type of competition. Thus the setting for the day of the six man bobsled showdown.

It was a beautiful cold sunny day when we arrived at my aunt and uncles, in Holland, Michigan. We had pulled in shortly after lunch. After kisses and hugs we settled in for the overnight visit. Our cousins asked if they could take us sledding at the hill. Our moms said that it would be ok, and to be home for dinner time at 7:00 p.m. We grabbed the sleds, saucers, big toboggan and headed out. A couple of blocks from their house the city had blocked off a street with a big hill, for the local kids to use for riding their sleds down. This hill had somewhat of a steep angle you could pick up some speed on. The surface conditions were perfect for sledding that day. At the bottom of the hill the snow was piled up quite high from the road being plowed, so the cars could get through. That pile of snow looked to be roughly seven to eight feet tall. After a time of going up and down the hill, someone had the bright idea, and came up with the six man bobsled competition. Not only did we have a big toboggan, but a couple of other kids also had one. The rules were simple, who ever went the farthest with six guys on the sled would be the winner. Of course there was no trophies or prizes, only the privilege of telling everyone at school that you were the winners.

Teams were set up and now it was time for a group to step up and take the first turn. After much time had passed we spoke up and said that we would be the first sled to go. If you have ever see a bobsled race on TV, you know that when they take off, all would push the sled to get it started and then each person would jump in the sled to take off. We were a little different. We put the lightest guy in the sled first and then proceeded to push him, while

53

the next guy would jump on the sled. This was done with the biggest kid jumping in last. By the time the last guy was on the sled we had picked up quite a bit of speed going down the hill. With all six of us guys moving at a fast clip, the bottom was coming up fast. I am sure that we all were thinking the same thing. Do we bail out and cut the distance on the length of our ride? Do we just sit tight and run it out as far as we can and hope we don't hit that hard packed snow pile? No one yelled out what to do, so the unspoken consensuses, was to hang on and run it out. Suddenly we had reached the point of no return regarding the snow pile next to the street, it was too late to bail. Someone said to hang on and the next thing I knew we were airborne. Yes all six of us was in the middle of the plowed street in the air. In a flash we had landed just short of the pile on the other side of the road. When that toboggan hit the hard pavement with all of us hanging on to it and each other, it just exploded into what looked like small pieces of wood! With all of us laying in the road, one of us busted out laughing and then the rest of us started to laugh also, with the exception of Rick. We got up and went over to check on Ricky and he was not moving. Someone said is he all right. I am sure that we were all thinking is he dead. One of us then bent down and turned Ricky over. He broke out in a smile and said "I got all of you suckers". After that we all stared busting out laughing again and started chatting about the ride down the hill we just had. At the end of the challenge we did win the showdown, because the other challengers would bail out before coming to the bottom of the hill. On the way home we had to draw straws to see who would have the pleasure of telling our mothers about the exploded toboggan.

When I think back on this winter day and the visit I had with my relatives, I wonder what the Lord will have me learn about this. Is He reminding me that family will not always be there? Is the Lord telling us that we will only have eternal life through Him? Do we remember that He is always sitting on the toboggan of life, with us on this earth? So the question is, do you have Jesus riding down that hill with you?

21 Pinball Wizard

The time era was around 1969 and I was in the tenth grade of high school. My brother had talked me into skipping school that day. It was a beautiful day, the sun was shining and it was a nice cool fall day. Now this was the first time I ever skipped a day of school, let alone miss one for being sick. If I remember that last day of school I missed was when I was thirteen and had my tonsils removed. They told me that after I had them taken out while I was in the hospital, I could have all of the ice cream I wanted. Yeah right, but that is another story.

Ok on with the skipping school day. It was early in the morning and mom had woke us up and told us to get ready for school. By the time we had gotten dressed and eating breakfast mom and dad had left for work. Our walk to catch the bus was only about a quarter mile from the house. At the time we lived on a dead end street and all of the kids had to walk to the end of the road to catch the bus to school. Right before we started to head out of the house my little brother started hounding me about skipping school. He said that we could take some of our quarters and go to the local pool hall where they also had pin ball machines and have a good time. After not giving it much thought to the kind of trouble I would get into, I agreed to miss school that day.

After walking to town which was about a mile and half away we ended up in the pool hall shooting pool and playing pinball. Of course being a little gun shy, about after an hour the door of the small pool hall opened up. The first thought in my mind was great, I have been busted and I will be getting in trouble with my parents and the school. Walking in the door and much to my surprise, it was our cousins from Holland, Michigan. Call it a consequence but it was a shock that they showed up and decided to skip school the same day we did. Now my older cousin Junior had just gotten a nice used 1967 Plymouth Road runner car, and they decided to skip school and come down our way for a ride. Of course when they saw the pool hall sign with all of the pinball machines inside they had to stop. After giving high fives, playing pinball, shooting pool and picking at each other we all jumped into the car to go for a ride looking to see what other things we could do.

Now living close to Benton Harbor, there was a place called the Old House of David. It was a place where you could somewhat call an amusement park back in that day. They had a small train for rides around the park. There was a small museum, some small shops selling different types of items, along with restaurants, etc. Also there was the big penny arcade building with several types of old mechanical machines to collect your change. The arcade was the place that we five boys were headed to. After a few hours in the arcade with all of us exhausting the money we had it was time to head home. Our cousins had to get back to Holland, Michigan, before school was let out. On their way home Junior dropped us off near the original pool hall that we met them at. My brother and I had a little time to kill before the bus would make its drop off of the other kids at the end of our dead end road. We decided to walk a few blocks to see if we could pick up some pop bottles to return to the neighborhood store for the deposit to buy a snack and eat it on the way home.

After timing it just right we were less than a hundred yards from the school bus stop at the end of our road, when the bus was leaving. As my brother and I were walking home we talked about how good of a time we had hanging out with cousins the whole day. We were only home about thirty minutes when our mother came home from work. Mom asked us how our day was at school, and we said fine. She then asked us, if we had fun hanging out with our cousins from Holland, Michigan for the day. About that time my throat swelled up and I could hardly swallow. After confessing to our mother of skipping school and what we had done that day, I knew we were heading for some kind of disciplinary action. Of course at that age it would not be a spanking. I wish it would have been, for the punishment would be over quickly. I am sure that our mother would discipline us with something that would make us think twice about skipping school again. And to this day after that I never skipped school again.

Now days, being a Christian, I think about what the Lord is having me learn by thinking of this time back then. I must remember to be a person that is honest and not try to hide any of the things I do from Him. The Lord is always there with me, even when I do not think I am being watched He is looking right at me. Christ wants me to be a man of integrity, without deceit, honest and pure to Him and others. So the question I have for myself and you, is what road will you want to travel? Does our road take us to school, or do we chose the road that leads to the pool hall?

22 Demon Squirrel

Have you ever had that feeling that someone, or something was watching your every move you were making? You know that kind of feeling when you would look over your shoulder to see if somebody was behind you. You would keep looking out of the corner of your eyes to see if something was close to you. After a while you would be so freaked out that it was time to leave the area and head someplace else.

I can remember the first time we dropped our one and only daughter off to the New Tribes Bible College. This was a small bible college in Jackson, Michigan. It was only about a two hour drive to the east from our home in southwest Michigan. In the back of our pickup truck, we had packed up, everything that our daughter Amy wanted to take for the college school year, which seemed like everything but the kitchen sink. I guess she thought she would need all of the stuff in the back of the truck and her loaded car. After securing down the load and covering it with a tarp, away we went. The trip took over three hours with having to stop and have lunch and double checking the load. Of course we had to stop and fill our daughter's gas tank in her car, pick up a few groceries and other items. Mom had to make sure that she had the additional items. We then made a quick stop at Wally-World, aka Walmart and pick up some items Amy also needed. After a period of time we finally made it to the college. Our daughter informed me that I would not be able to go to the girl's dorm to move her stuff in it because no men were allowed. With a smile on my face I said that is totally fine. I told her that I would stay by the truck and car to help them unload. In my mind I was thinking great this would be less work in moving stuff for me. I disliked moving very much probably due to the fact we moved around a lot when I was a kid, but that is another story. Amy and Mom grabbed some stuff and said that they would be back with some other girls to help unload the vehicles.

As I sat on the tailgate of the pickup truck waiting for all of the ladies to come back I notice out of the corner of my eye a big bushy tail red squirrel. At the present moment I did not even pay attention to the squirrel. A brief thought ran through my mind of that squirrel in the frying pan with some fresh biscuits and gravy. While waiting for my wife and the girls to come back, I decided to take a short walk around the dorm building. It was not too big of a building and only had about five floors to it. As I was walking down the side walk a crazy red squirrel was following me. I would stop and turn around and it would stop and stare at me. I would then turn back around and start walking and then it would start to follow me. This went on for a little while. Every time that squirrel would stop and look at me, I swear he was looking into my eyes of my soul. This squirrel was starting to freak me out a little. After seeing all of the girls at the truck from a distance, it was time to head back and get it unloaded.

Amy had managed to round up about six young ladies and they all made quick work of getting everything into her dorm room. By that time it was dinner time and Mom had to take her out for dinner and another run to Wally-World for something. My wife and I were waiting for Amy to come back to the truck, to go to dinner. As we were sitting on the tailgate waiting for our daughter, I began to tell my wife about the squirrel. Of course this little critter was in a tree next to where we were parked and watching us all of the time. After I told my wife of the story of the squirrel following me and staring me down when I went for a short walk earlier, my wife busted out laughing and started making fun of me. Shortly after that Amy came out and said that she had to go to the office and check about something for registration. We told her to take her time and we would be waiting here for her when she was finished.

After that my wife said she was going to take a short walk around the building, and check out the area a little bit. As she left I looked up in the tree and the squirrel was gone. I figured he must have seen what all the commotion was about and then left. A little while after my wife had left for her stroll, I saw her walking at a very quick pace on the way back to the truck I noticed the red squirrel following about ten yards behind her. When she had got back to the truck, she did not even stop at the tailgate but went directly to the passenger side of the pickup and jumped, in the truck closing the door behind her. I then went to the driver's side jumped in behind the wheel. With a smile on my face I asked her what was up. She then proceeded to tell me about the squirrel, which she called demon possessed. I let out a big laugh and reminded her that she called me crazy earlier about that squirrel. Shortly after that our daughter had come back to the truck and we all went out for dinner. After dinner we dropped Amy off at college and headed home.

On the way home my wife and I started talking and laughing about that so called demon possessed squirrel. I told her about the squirrel frying in the pan. She said she would have even made the biscuits and gravy to go with it. Now my wife is a good biscuit maker from way back and I told her we could have biscuits and gravy for breakfast in the morning. Of course she had to make biscuits the next morning that resembled squirrels, to go with the gravy for breakfast.

After giving this some thought, I was thinking, was this squirrel only protecting its family? Was the squirrel protecting its food source for himself and his family to last the winter? Or was the squirrel possibly rabid and trying to protect itself from harm? As a parent, would I not do basically the same thing? The Lord has made us all different from the animals in the world, but He has also given us some instincts that are similar. The question my wife and I were discussing on the way home in the pickup truck, do we go to the Lord when we are in fear of something, or somebody and let Him fight that battle for us? When we jump into the truck do we turn it over to God? Are we allowing the Lord to take control of our lives to provide our needs? Do we put Jesus center stage? Only the Father knows our hearts? Does Jesus know your heart?

23 Made To Last

The other day we were driving down I94 and I came across a 1957 Chevy, with the chrome glistening in the sunlight. It reminded me of a time when my parents had a blue one that looked almost just like it. Of course now days they seem to be a little smaller looking, then when I was a young boy. Then again compared to the cars made today that 57 is still a giant.

Sometimes I remind my kids unlike today with the car seats for the small children the only car seat that I had as a child was when my parents told me to sit down, shut up and hold on. When I think and look at things today, I am puzzled at how there is not much pride, quality and dependability of things that are made in our world today. We have truly turned into a society with disposable items. Although according to my wife one of the greatest inventions for a young mother was the disposal diaper. That one is a little hard to argue with.

In the time back, I remember the inside of the barn on the homestead and all of the little coffee cans, jars and containers my dad had filled with various screws, nails, washers, etc. I asked him one day why he was saving all of that junk and he said, "Son you never know when you may need that one size bolt or washer". Little did I realize that he probably was seeing the change to a disposal world a whole lot earlier than me? Besides that he was a millwright in his trade and he always had to come up with creative ways to get the machines going. Back then a person had to make things happen with what they had to work with. Even if it meant to dig that dry well by hand! As I get older I have learned from the old saying. Learn to work smarter not harder, even if it is having those boys dig that drywell by hand. Thanks Dad!

I can remember back in the early 70's when my one brother bought a little foreign made pickup truck. It was brand new with less than twenty miles on it. I think he said that he only paid about $2800.00 dollars for it. The truck was yellow in color and almost too small for this big guy to get into. About a month after he had bought the new truck, all of us boys were at my parents' house for a visit. Of course all of us were outside with dad and talking about some of the design of the latest vehicles coming out on the market. As we were looking at my one brother's new yellow truck, we noticed that there was a slight brown spot near the back wheel well. Of course we joked with him and told him he needed to wash it once in a while. My brother made the comment that he when through the car wash before he came over to my parents' house. As all five us gather around the back of the truck and started taking a closer look at the brown spot, we came to the conclusion that it was rust. Needless to say that the one brother was not too happy about his new truck starting to rust. Of course back then they did not have a very good warranty. Any way he did not keep it to long before he traded it off.

Sometimes I look at the world and all of the sin in it and I think of all the lost ones that are living the disposable life. If only they would realize that the Lord is there for them to accept Him and then their lives will be made to last forever. I am thankful that the Lord is with me and now my life is made to last forever with Him. As Christians are we letting the Lord take care of the rust that comes into our lives? Do we allow that warranty He paid on the cross for us, to be the way He has made to last for us for eternity?

24 What's Important To Me!!!

As I look back at the trails that I have cut in the wilderness of this world I think of what was important to me. With that being said I look at how our lives seem to be getting busier as we get older. While reflecting back to the days of yesteryear, I think about the time I spent with my grandfather fishing, hunting, washing the car and something as simple as having a cool glass of ice tea to drink under the shade tree. My grandfather loved to fish and hunt. Sometimes we would go fishing all day and bring home a bucket of bluegill or crappie. The first thing my grandmother would do would get a pan of salt water ready and a couple of knives. After we unloaded the row boat and put all of the fishing equipment up we would join my grandmother in the back yard and help her finish cleaning the fish. You see my grandparents were from the old school and my grandmother would not even hesitate to clean fish, rabbits, squirrels, pheasants, or any other wild game that was brought home. My grandfather would make the comment sometimes while we were cleaning the wild game, "Pierce, make sure that you marry a woman that is willing to stand by your side and do what she has to do to help take care of her family". Often I would catch my grandmother with a little smile on her face when he said that.

One day my grandfather and I were having that glass of tea under that shade tree and he proceeded to give me some advice again at my young age. I don't know why, but my grandfather hardly ever called me by my first name. He would always call me by my last name Pierce. I don't ever remember him calling any of his other grandsons by their last names when we were all together. I guess that was his way of treating me a little special. It took me a few years to figure this out. Anyway, one of the things that he said to me was, "Pierce, as you go through life son, remember one thing, any job worth doing is worth doing right". At the time I did not fully understand what he meant by this.

Now that I am older and I think of some of the times that my grandfather and I spent together, I reflect on some of the things that he had told me. Some of these things I also try to pass along to my children and now grandchildren as they come along. I can still hear him in my ear of some of the projects (jobs) that I even do today. Pierce, any job worth doing is worth doing right. I am thankful that I did marry a woman that will stand by me and do what she has to do to take care of our family. But please note she is not into cleaning wild game, which I may bring home. I am sure that if she had too she would.

To wrap it up, it was important to my grandparents to take the time to give me the advice that they felt was important to them and help turn me into the type of man I am today. They say the grandparents of a child have a bigger influence on them than their parents. I do truly believe this statement. With my grandparent's advice and the direction from the Lord, it has made me come to the realization of how some things are important to all of us. Going forward, I need to make sure that my children and grandchildren are shown of how important that God is to me. A challenge to all of us, is what is the Lord making important in our lives so we can pass it onto our family?

25 Pheasant Hunting

I was around the age of 13 years old. It was fall time and the hunting season had started. My grandfather was an avid hunter and introduced me to the sport. That time of the year he would be in the woods from sun up to sun down. One of his most favorite things to hunt were pheasants. My grandfather had a well-trained hunting dog. This dog was one of his most prized possession. It seemed like that dog would be at his side everywhere he went.

It was the opening day of small game season in southwest Michigan. My grandfather had given me a single shot 20 gage shot gun to use for hunting season. Granddad had said the best way to learn to shoot accurately is with a single shot shotgun. You will learn faster knowing that you only had one shot at a time. Along with the shotgun he gave me the gun case and a box of shells. Grandad told me the next box I would have to buy when I ran out. He suggested that I make each shell count. It was now time to head for the hunting grounds.

After loading up our gear and the dog we drove to a nearby farmers land that my grandfather had permission to hunt on. It was a cool fall day and there was a slight frost on the weeds and grass in the open fields. It was a good thing we had been well dressed for hunting or our clothes would have been wet from the frost. Soon we made our way to the hunting grounds where the pheasants were supposed to be plentiful. My grandfather gave the command to his hunting dog to start working the fields, trying to flush out a male ring neck pheasant. Within about thirty minutes that old dog flushed out a big beautiful female hen. According to the state of Michigan hunting rules you cannot kill a female pheasant. The females were protected so that there could be more pheasants born for restocking of the males that were killed during hunting season.

When the pheasant took flight after the dog flushed it out we both raised our guns ready to shoot. My grandad yelled out the word hen and then I knew I could not take a shot at the female pheasant. Again both of us, along with the dog, started again to work the big open field looking for a big male ring neck pheasant. What seemed like a short period of time and an even shorter walk that old bird dog flushed out a male pheasant. My gun went up and I took the shot and missed. Within a second my grandfather took a shot and nailed the bird. The bird dog then retrieved the slain pheasant and delivered it to my grandfather. Granddad then looked at me smiled and then said, "Practice makes perfect".

One of the things that I believe the Lord was teaching me on this hunting trip was to gain experience, knowledge and rely on Him. Sometimes we have only that one shot to accomplish the work the good Lord wants us to do. The questions we can ask ourselves is have we taken the time to gain that experience, knowledge and are we relying on Him? Practice does make perfect when we are witnessing for our Savior. Are you willing to put the time in to make that one shot count? Only Jesus knows the answer along with you.

26 Raking Leaves Fun or Work?

As I was driving west on Red Arrow Highway going home from work I came across several people in their yards raking leaves. I even spotted a couple of little children out raking and putting the leaves in a pile. Were they going to use the pile to make a fort, or maybe use it to hide in? Possibly they were just making a pile to jump in. Who knows what was going through their imaginations. The work of raking the leaves to them had turned into fun rather than a chore. When you were a child, it was almost impossible to not jump into the middle of a pile of leaves when you came across one. These days if I were to jump in the middle of a pile of leaves, someone would have to call 911 to get me out of it.

The work of gathering all of the leaves in my yard and into one spot sometimes seems like it is nearly impossible with the wind blowing them all over the place. Along with the wind comes the fact there were more leaves falling off the trees. When I was younger I would tackle the duty of raking the leaves to one area of the yard for disposal. Again I would fight the wind and the other leaves falling off of the trees. Sometimes I would look back on a spot that I had already raked and it looked just like it did before I started. Determined to make the yard look better I would go back and start all over again. Again the chore had begun of clearing the area that I had already completed.

Now that I have gotten older I have learned to work smarter and not harder. I think at some point in our lives we truly discover what this phrase actually means and learn from it. Of course for and old hard head like me, it probably took a little while longer than some others. With that being said I have learned to work a little smarter, like check the wind conditions, take smaller sections to work on and always rake with the wind not against the wind.

While I was driving the thought came into my head. We are like the leaves. The Lord has the power to calm the wind and gather us together. He can protect us from things that harm, scatter and even deliver us from disposal. All we have to do is open our hearts to Him. One of these days I will again be able to jump into that pile of leaves, without somebody calling 911 to get me out. And if they do dial 911, the Lord will be there to take me by the hand.

27 Working Co-Op

Back when I attended high school there was a program for kids called Co-Op. This was a type of program that a high school student could earn high school credits while working at an approved job. I have always thought that this was a great thing and it gave a chance for young people to learn about all things in relation to getting and keeping a job. Most all of the employers were on board with this program. It gave them a chance to mentor and groom possible future employees.

In my senior year of high school I was able to be a co-op student. I would go to school for a couple of hours in the morning when school started and then go to work after that. Now when I was going to high school they had it set up that, the seniors and juniors would go to school in the morning from about seven a.m. to noon, with the sophomores and freshmen going in the afternoon. The school that I went to was a big school with four hundred eighty six students in my graduating class alone. It was good to be able to leave school and go right to work and pick up a couple of dollars to put in your pocket while getting credits applied for school to count for being able to graduate.

Ok the company that I worked for was a small organization that cleaned work uniforms, shop towels, rugs, etc. I was trained to do various types of jobs within the company. I would do things like fold and package shop towels, run a uniform pressing machine, run different types of commercial washing machines and dryers. I even learned how to run different types of dry cleaning machines. I learned quite a bit while working for this company for almost a year. I remember the first week I was working I was taking some blue work uniforms out of a dry cleaning machine and putting them in a basket to be taken to the pressing machine, when I noticed, something in the basket of the machine. The baskets on these types of machines were quite large in size. They were big enough for a person to climb into.

After reaching into the back of the basket which took up almost half of my body, I discovered a fifty dollar bill. I took the bill to by supervisor, Mr. Smith, to give to him. My supervisor said that this happens all of the time. Mr. Smith explained to me that sometimes guys, who rented the uniforms would put money in their pocket and forget about it. He told me that the procedure was, to put the money in an envelope with my name and date on it and after one week if no one called to claim the money he would give it back to me and I was able to keep it. When it was break time, I talked with some of my co-workers and they said that you would fine all types of things that people would forget about and leave in their pockets. Some of these would be tools, rings, pictures, paper money and especially coins. While working there it seemed like someone was finding money all of the time. I think that I was able to collect over two hundred dollars for the short period of time that I was employed there. I truly believe that this was a good program to teach young adults, some of the responsibilities of being in the work force. I am not sure if schools are doing this type of program today. If not then in my opinion it needs to be brought back.

As I think back on this time in my working career, I wonder what the Lord, has taught me. I could have put that fifty dollar bill in my pocket and not said anything, but if you do the right thing He will bless you and your cup will run over. By giving the boss the money found, it shows that you are an honest employee. It shows that you are a person of integrity and good character. It also shows that you are the type of person who could handle a promotion within the organization. When we are at that fork in the road we need to take the one way that leads to doing the right thing. Even when it is a tougher road to walk on He will bless us abundantly.

28 Gas Jockey

Remember when there was a time when we had Gas Jockey's? Now for those youngsters, of you that do not know what a Gas Jockey is, it is a person who would pump gas in your car and do other small related things for you at the gas pump. I remember it, like it was yesterday. I was about sixteen years old and worked at a Phillip's 66 gas station in the Fairplain plaza. Some of the other duties of a gas Jockey were checking tire pressure, checking engine fluid levels and washing your windshield. A lot of the older cars back then had the gas fill tube behind the back license plate. Of course the pickup trucks had them by the driver door. Anyway there were different fill spots on different types of vehicles. Other responsibilities of being a Gas Jockey was to make sure that the gas islands and the service station was kept clean and in order.

You may not believe it but the price of gas was around thirty one cent a gallon, give or take a few pennies. I believe I was making around eighty five cents an hour. The guy's name that I worked for was Ed Gunn. Ed was a very fair boss to work for. He would often buy me lunch or a snack if we worked together. I can remember one day Ed had to leave early and take care of some personal business. Ed asked if I would be OK and be able to fly solo. Anyway he felt that it was time for me to run the ship alone. Back in those days there were no cell phones, only land lines. Ed said he would give me a call later to see how it was going.

Everything was going fine until about an hour after Ed left. All of a sudden it seemed like everybody decided to get gas at the same time. On the gas islands there were four pumps, two for regular and two for high test. The high test gasoline was a better grade of regular with a higher octane. The unleaded gasoline had not been invented at that time. Of course it seemed like forever there was car after car that wanted to be filled. The nice thing was that not very many people wanted some of the other services, just a fill up. A good Gas Jockey would be able to keep those four pumps going all at the same time.

After a little while the stream of cars coming in had slowed down. By then I had worked up a sweat from all of the running. I had went inside the service station to unload some of the money in my pocket into the cash register when the phone ringed. It was my boss Ed. He asked me what I was up too and that he had been calling for the last twenty minutes. I told him that we got swamped for a little while with everybody wanting gas. He laughed and said he knew, because he drove by the station. Ed told me to hang on that he would be back in to work in about fifteen minutes. When Ed came in he told me that I did a good job, brought in a little snack and bought me a cold drink out of the soda machine.

What are some of the life lessons that the Lord our Savior has shown me from this time of being a Gas Jockey? Would you say that being patience in a tough time will pay off? Being clam in the storm and keeping your ship (Self) on course, help you weather the storm you are in? Does putting a smile on your face when you are face to face with adversity help you maintain sanity? Will you totally rely on Jesus, for carrying you when the chips are down in your day? Can you fill your tank (Heart) with the High Test (Jesus) to get through the chaotic day? Which will you choose Regular, or High Test?

29 Saving Grandma

We were invited over to the folks for a Sunday dinner. After getting the car back from the body shop, all of us were packed into that little 1985 Ford Escort. The car in the body shop is another story in its self. At the time all three of the kids were under nine years old and fit in the back seat. We were going to meet some of the other family members there and all of us were looking forward to a good time. It was a beautiful fall day and all of the trees were turning different shades of red, orange, and yellows.

We pulled into my parents driveway and the leaves here flying in a small whirlpool motion off of the ground. All of the kids were excited to see this. They exited the car and were able to run through the flying leaves a few times before it stopped. They asked how there could be a little tornado like that. I told them it was probably caused from the position of their grandparent's house and garage with the wind blowing into them. Well after a couple of minutes it was time to go in to get hugs and kisses, from Grandma.

After a little while some of the other family members showed up for the Sunday afternoon dinner. After all of the kids received their routine kisses and hugs, we shooed them outside to play before dinner was ready. The ladies had retreated to the kitchen to get the food ready while the fellows hung out in the living room to watch the football game.

The ladies had been setting up the table along with putting some of the food on it, when I walked by and it looked like Grandma was choking on something at the table. I asked her if she was alright and she shook her head no and grabbed her throat. Remembering the Heimlich maneuver from my recent first aid training, I yelled for help and sprang into action. I reached my arms around Grandma's waist and gave a quick squeeze. At first nothing happened so I gave her a bigger squeeze the next time. It worked, because a big green olive flew out of her mouth and she took a big deep breath of air. Someone got her a chair and she was able to set down. With tears streaming down her cheek, we asked if she was alright and she said that she was and just

73

needed a little time to compose herself. Grandma set there for a little while and let the girls finish getting the Sunday dinner ready.

It was dinner time and all of the kids had come in being hungry and ready to eat. After grace was said and thanking the Lord for Grandma being OK, we dug in and started to enjoy the food. Of course Uncle Carl had to ask Grandma if she would like some green olives to eat. As usual he got the look. You know that look that all mothers give you when you do something you should not have. The look that all women are born with. I have seen that look several times in my life, but that's another story. I can truly say that since Grandma has passed away, I even still miss that look.

After dinner and we all settled in at Grandma and Grandpa's house for the afternoon. The kids when back outside to play. The fellows, went to finish watching the ball game. Grandma and the girls went in the kitchen to clean up. Uncle Daniel reminded Grandma to stay away from the green olives. Once again Grandma gave that look and it sent chills all down our spines.

Looking back at that day, I think of what the Lord blessed us with. He taught us that life is precious and had given us more time to be with Grandma on earth. He taught us that family will not always be around and that we need to enjoy and look out after each other. Take the time to be with one and another. Yes even the green olive is as mighty as the sword. Praise the Lord that we could have a little more time with Grandma.

30 Eighty Miles A Hour

It was a nice spring day and I decided to take the three kids over to visit a friend of mine and help him work on building his home. At the build site would be his son the kids could play with while we were working on his house. Of course we would put the kids to work on picking up trash and sweeping the floors. While there the kids could go exploring into the woods, play ball, run in the apple orchards and other fun things a kid could do.

Now Lee lived about twelve miles from our home out in the rural area of southwest Michigan. After packing the kids, tools, cooler and picnic basket of lunch my wife had fixed for us into the 1974 Chevy El Camino, away we went. It was a beautiful ride on the back country roads to where we were going. There would be apple, cherry and peach trees with the colorful blossoms on them. There would be fields, with the earth just plowed that the farmers were getting ready to plant. What a nice warm spring day it had turned out to be for our drive over there.

On the way we went with all of us packed into the front of the El Camino it was a little tight. To settle down the kids I turned the radio on and we listen for songs to sing while on the way to our building destination. After a while of cruising and listening to the radio while in route, my daughter Amy whom was sitting right next to me noticed that I had reached the speed of over sixty five miles an hour. I remember hearing her say "dad you are going over sixty five miles an hour". Of course the next words out of her mouth were, "I am going to tell mom". Then the two boys said, "Yea we are going to tell mom that you were speeding down the road". I just laughed and told them to go ahead and tell your mother all of you little tattle tales. I told them to just go ahead and tell the world, that I did not even care.

We had finally reached my buddies house he was building. We said our hellos and started to unload the tools. Lee took the kids and put them to work moving some trash to a burn site he had set up. After that he came back and we started on running the wiring for the house. After a couple of hours we had the kids move

75

inside the house and put them to work, sweeping and organizing some things inside. Soon after that the kids were done with their work and we sent them outside to play. I told them to stay around because in a little while we would have lunch. Lee and I went back to working on the wiring and breaking a sweat from the warm spring day.

The time had passed by quickly and the kids had shown back up. They were dirty and hungry as Lee and I were also dirty and hungry. We all went to the back of the old El Camino opened up the picnic basket and cooler to have lunch. Grace was said and we all started to dig in. Fortunately mom had packed us sandwiches, chips, potato salad, apple slices, and some other goodies. We also had a cooler of water and soda. There was enough for all to have seconds if you wanted them. After lunch the kids went off to do some exploring into the woods, and Lee and I went back to working on the house.

The late afternoon had come upon us, and it was time to head back home. We gave a yell for the kids to come back from the woods. After packing up the El Camino, we said our good byes and made our way back home. On the way home I remembered what the kids said about going over the speed limit and doing sixty five miles an hour. I told them to hold on to their hats I was going to crank the car up to eighty miles an hour. Mike said, "We are going to tell mom and you will be in trouble". I told Amy to watch the speedometer, because here we go. Back in those days of the muscle car era, most of the vehicles had eight cylinder motors, and you could get up to eighty miles an hour very quickly. After pressing down on the gas pedal, the old El Camino got up to eighty miles an hour very quickly. Being a heavy cars like they were back then, when I let off of the gas, the car slowed down to fifty five pretty rapidly. It seemed like all three of the kids were in unison, when they said, "We are going to tell mom". I just laughed and told them to go ahead.

Soon we were back home and all three of them went running into the house. While unloading the El Camino, I could hear them singing like canaries to their mother about me going eighty miles an hour. Shortly after that I went into the house and all of the kids were standing by mom. Out of the corner of my eye I could see big smiles like dad, you are in big trouble now from all of the kids. Mom gave me a wink and said, "I heard you were speeding, and going over eighty miles an hour on the road today". I told her yes I was, and asked, did she hear it from my three little tattle tales, that sing like little canaries? Mom just winked back at me and said, "She heard about it from a little birdy". I just smiled and told mom that I had heard of that little birdy.

It had been a good day and I think that all of the kids and even my buddy's kid learned a couple of things that day, while working on his house. After reflecting back on this time, I think of what lessons the Lord wants me to learn. Is it, we cannot hide our sins from Him? Is it He is looking over us at all times? Could it be, He is there with each of us in the old El Camino with only one seat, going eighty miles an hour? The question I have for you, is Jesus, the little birdy, looking out after you? I pray He is.

31 Rock 'in The Boat

It all happened shortly after we decided to go on an adult camping and canoe trip being organized at our church we attended. Someone had the great idea of having this trip for adults to get away from their children and have a time of fellowship with other adults in the church. After being able to find someone to care for our three kids, we were looking forward to the getaway. It was in the time era when we had that 1974 Chevy El Camino. It was also around the time period of the eighty miles an hour with little birdies, but that is another story. Both my wife and I were looking forward to getting away for a couple of days.

Well it was Friday morning and we had just dropped the kids off at the sitter for the weekend. We were on the way back to the house to park the car and pick up the loaded El Camino with all of our camping gear. All we had to do was switch out vehicles and head to the church parking lot where all of us were meeting. On the way to the church we stopped by the convenience store to grab a couple of sodas for celebrating, the beginning of the time away from three children. Don't get me wrong we truly love our kids, but it was nice to get some time for ourselves.

After arriving at church we were surprised to see how many other couples were there, eager and ready to go. There must have been about thirty or more of us. We were going to a private camp ground only about seventy miles away. This was a nice place that had indoor restrooms and even hot showers available. The price of camping was very affordable, at this private camp ground. Prayer was asked, then we all lined up and formed a convoy to get to the camp grounds.

After everybody pulled into their assigned camp sites we started to unload the El Camino and set up our tent. After a short period of time my wife and I had completed staging our area, of the campsites. Our tent was ready with all of the items in it that needed to be there, our coolers were in place and we had a small fire going in the fire pit. After just sitting down in our lawn chairs

78

we were told to assemble at one of the team leader's site for an informational meeting.

It was getting close to supper time and we headed to the team leaders camp site for a meeting. At the meeting we were given an itinerary and other related materials regarding our canoe trip and stay at the adult camp out. Now my wife just loved this. She is a list kind of person. On the itinerary was the times and places we need to be for the meals and all activities. We would be going on the canoe trip in the morning. Back at the camp ground during lunch we would then have a time of fellowship with each other. There was even a time scheduled for quite time and studying God's word. All in all we were set up with all kinds of things to do. It looked like we were going to have a lot of fun with the different things on the list. One of my favorites was the chance to pitch some horseshoes. This reminded me of a time when a buddy of mine and I won the horseshoe contest at a camp ground years ago. But that is another story.

After the short meeting it was time to get set up for the dinner hour. Taking on the work of cooking for about thirty campers was no easy task. Again the old saying of many hands make light work comes into effect. Some of the men, started to assemble the picnic tables in rows. Other gents started to get the fire ready to cook on. A couple of guys set down some cinder blocks around the camp fire. Another two fellows moved a three foot by five foot steel plate onto the cinder blocks. It was funny to watch the four of them trying to make sure that the steel plate was nice and level. The steel plate was the one we used in a church camp out that had three men and twenty one boys. But then again that is another story.

I looked over and saw a pair of gentlemen digging a hole with shovels. Being curious I had to go over and asked what was going on. Jim said that we were going to roast corn in the dirt pit. Now if you never had seen this done, it is something to see. What you do is shovel out a dirt pit about the size of four foot in width and five foot in length. You then will need to dig down about one foot in depth. After putting a layer of hot coals from the fire pit into the hole, you would lay down a layer of wet burlap bags. You would then put a layer of the sweet corn that had been soaking in cool water for a few hours with the husk still on them, on top of the wet sacks. After that you would cover the corn with more wet sacks. Be sure that the corn is very well protected inside the layers of wet burlap both on the top and bottom to prevent any dirt from getting on the corn. After the corn is completely covered and protected with the wet bags you would shovel a thin layer of dirt on top of the wet bags that are covering the corn. In about an hour the corn will be cooked and ready to serve.

The ladies had been busy getting some of the other food prepared to be cooked on the grill or in the fire. There were a couple of cast iron pots full of baked beans ready to be put in the fire pit along with hamburger patties, hotdogs and brats to throw on the grill. Potato salad, coleslaw and other goodies were being set out on the picnic tables. Paper plates, cups, ice tea, condiments and all types of fixings were getting set on the tables. Fortunately the ladies, had a lot of stuff made in advance of the camping trip, which was kept in the coolers waiting for their time to be served. As I was walking by the fire pit I saw a one gallon jar of something being heated by the fire. I asked what it was and Bill said that it was the butter for the corn. He then explained to me how it will butter our sweet corn. What it was, is a gallon jar which was half filled with water and half filled with butter. You would peel the husk back on your corn and dip it into the warm water and butter. You would then pull it out slowly to coat the corn with the butter floating on top of the water. I thought it was a great idea.

What seemed like only a couple of minutes, it was time to dig up the corn and remove all of the other cooked items in the pots and on the grill. The asking of the blessing on the food was completed and we all lined up to dig in. After dinner and everything was cleaned up it was time for a bible study and fellowship around the fire. We all retrieved our lawn chairs and bibles, for a great evening of praising the Lord and talking about His word. Soon it was time to hit the sack and get rested up for the planned canoe trip the next day. After my wife and I hit the sack I got to thinking about the great dinner that night with the dessert of s'mores around the fire. I can only imagine how the morning breakfast was going to be.

After a night of some sleep in our tent I remembered how that old ground was still as hard as ever. I got up and took a walk over to the mess hall area to see what was going on. Luckily someone had started a couple pots of coffee going. After getting a cup of java and stretching the old bones I was beginning to move better. After a while most of our group had risen and was looking forward to breakfast. The cooks had started breakfast on top of that steel plate. On the menu were fried potatoes with onions, eggs, biscuits, sausage links and other related condiments. As I was watching the guys cook the breakfast and those eggs sliding around on the steel plate I remembered why they were working so hard to get that plate nice and level. After breaking the eggs open onto the cured plate, if it was not good and level the eggs would have slid right off of it. There were no edges to keep the food from going over the side on that steel plate. It did amaze me how they got that three by five foot grill so well cured that the food would not stick to it.

Shortly after breakfast there was a small group devotion and then it was time to get ready for the two hour canoe trip. We had all moved to the campground office building, where we would need to pay for the canoe rental for the trip. Everyone loaded onto a school bus and were driven a few miles down the road to where the canoe launch area was. After a few directions from the campground director we took off. While we were floating down the river with enjoying the scenery, wildlife and watching some of the other group members, my wife and I were having a great time.

Soon we had reached our final destination at the receiving area of the campgrounds we were stationed at. Our canoe was one of the last ones to reach the unloading spot. While we were waiting for the couple ahead of us to get out of their canoe and make their way up the slippery bank, I told my wife that we would move our canoe onto the bank. I said to her, "I would then hold it steady so she could get out and then in turn she could hold it for me". If you have ever been in a canoe you know that when you stand up it is very easy to tip the canoe over and get a soaking. All was going well as my wife was getting out. I then asked her to steady the canoe so that I can make my way out of it. As I begin to stand up and get ready to step out of the canoe onto the side of the river bank I could hear and see my wife talking to a couple of the other ladies. All of a sudden she let go, just as my one foot was stepping over the edge. At that time with no one holding the canoe and me being a big guy the canoe slipped away from the bank and in the river I went!

As soon as I came up from underneath the water totally soaked, I stood up in the river and grabbed the canoe to keep it from floating down the river. My wife along with the rest of the group all busted out laughing at me. The next thing I did was pushed the canoe onto shore to make sure it would not float away and took off at a dead run for that wife of mine. She knew that I was about to get her wet by dragging her into the river. She shot up the side of the bank at an incredible speed and I was not able to catch her. Of course the rest of the group let out an even bigger chuckle at us than when I went into the water of the river. The next time I saw her was at our campsite when I went to get some dry clothes to put on.

Soon after drying off it was time to meet the group for lunch. Now guys will be guys and I heard the remarks from the other fellows around the camp fire the rest of the day. Being a good sport I just smiled at them and took it, with it all being in fun. After lunch we all fellowshipped by playing horseshoes, board games, cards, etc. That evening after what was another delicious campfire dinner we started to get ready to break camp and get some things packed and ready for the journey back home. That morning we all would go our separate ways back home. Hopefully we would get back in time to make it to the Sunday morning service at church.

After making it home and picking up the kids from the sitter we had just enough time to show up for the Sunday morning service at the church we attended. It looked like most of the other campers had made it also. The pastor greeted us in the foyer and asked how the drowned wet rat was doing. I knew at that time the news of me falling into the river had gotten around. I said to the pastor with a chuckle that I was now high and dry. We both laughed and then my wife and I headed to one of the pews in the sanctuary. Now in this day of technology it did not surprise me to see some pictures of the canoe trip on the overhead screen. As suspected there it was on the screen a picture of me standing in the river and being wet from head to toe. My wife just smiled and said that she was glad that I did not catch her running up the river bank. We both just laughed and said what a memory we had made.

All in all it was a great time to get away with my wife and enjoy the time to fellowship, with my Christian friends. What a great blessing to have someone trustworthy and able to watch our three children for a couple of days while we were away. It was one of those things that will forever be a lasting memory for both myself and my wife.

With this time of the adult canoe trip running through my mind I think of the lessons that the Lord is blessing me with. Was He teaching me to be humble and take the ribbing from my fellow Christians as a time of putting up crowns in heaven? Is He showing me to love my wife even when she is distracted and wanting to talk with others? Does the Lord want me to know that no matter what, I do have others that are willing to show that they enjoy my fellowship? Does He want me to know that He does have a sense of humor? Maybe the Lord was just showing me that as a Christian, we can still have a good time, while still walking in His will.

32 1st Time Campers

I remember back when our three children were around the ages of seven, eight and nine. It was around the fourth of July. Now my wife and the kids have never been camping before. We decided it was now the time they all learned some of the survival skills needed to live in the woods. Besides that the two boys were in cub scouts and they needed to work on some the badges earned as a cub scout. We decided to go to a state camp ground outside of Allegan, Michigan for the holiday weekend.

While in the process of getting the camping gear ready to load our youngest Amy started to cry and said that she did not want to go camping. When we asked her why she did not want to go all she would say is that she did not like camping. Her older brothers had probably messed with her and told her something like a bear or something in the woods would get her. After loading up the pickup and the car with enough camping equipment, food coolers, tents and of course bicycles for three kids and two adults, away we went. The spot we were going to was called Pine Point Campground. It was about an hour and fifteen minute drive from our home before we had finally reached our destination.

The camp ground was a small indiscreet area located on a small lake which had a little dam at one end to release some of the spring fed water from a nearby stream. Like most state campgrounds there was only a well pump and outdoor toilets. The out houses were the type when you got in you did your business and got out quickly, if you know what I mean. With it being a holiday weekend the campground was getting pretty well filled up by the time we got there. It always seemed like everybody would avoid the camp sites close to the out houses. I am pretty sure you can figure out why those camp sites were the last ones to be used.

The task of teaching camping and survival skills has now commenced and I told the family, aka troops, to start unloading the truck. I informed them the first task is to set up our tents. We did not have a big tent only a couple of pup tents. There was one for the two boys and one for myself, wife and daughter. With the completion of setting up the tents, it was time to make a fire. I told all of the troops that the boys and I would be looking for firewood in the nearby woods. After a time of explanation on the fine art of gathering fallen fire wood, into the woods the three of us went looking for the wood. I also told the boys to make sure they stayed within hearing distance of the campground so we would not get lost. While the two girls stayed at the camp site, their job was to finish unloading the truck and put the bedding into the tents.

The boys and I were not looking for firewood very long in the woods. We were fortunate enough to run across some old rotten fallen trees about seventy five yards from the camp site. I told the boys to pick up what they could carry so we could head back to camp. I told them that we could bring the axe and hand saw back later to get more wood. On the way back to the camp site I suggested to the boys that we think of an easier way to transport the wood back to the site. After making it back to the camp site it looked like the girls had unloaded most of the truck with the exception of some of the heavy items.

It was fire training time, and all of the troops assembled at the fire pit. After showing the group on how to set up the wood stack for the proper amount of air flow and kindling that was put under the wood logs it was time to fire it up. One of the boys asked if we were going to lite it with the technique of using a stick and rope. I asked the troops if they were hungry and wanted to try the rope and stick way or fire it up with some dry matches and get the hotdogs going. Their stomachs must have won the decision because they all selected the matches to get the fire going. I did tell them that you want to make sure that your matches stay dry all of the time for when you need to start a fire. This reminds me of another time when three of us men took a group of about twenty one boys from the church on an overnight camp out. But then again that is another story.

While the fire was burning down to a level you could cook on in the pit it was time to finish unloading the truck and setting up camp. We were close to being done with camp setup when I told the kids if they wanted to, they could take their bikes for a ride around the camp grounds and check out things. I told the boys to keep an eye on their sister and be back in about an hour for supper. They were all excited and off they went. My wife was a little nervous about this. I told her to relax and have faith that the Lord will watch over the kids. Taking a little break I sit down in a lawn chair and enjoyed the fire and the quietness of the woods that surrounded us. What seemed like only a couple of minutes, the fire had gotten to the point where we would now be able to grill the hotdogs.

We had opened up one of the coolers and took out some hotdogs, prepared potato salad and condiments. We put some blocks around the fire with a metal cooking grate on top of them over the hot coals. After that we opened up a can of baked beans, then put both items on the grill to start the cooking process. My wife set up the picnic table that was at the camp site with the potato salad, chips, plates, etc. When you have three kids that have been outside working and playing around you can image the amount groceries they can eat. This reminds me of a time when we had about eight boys overnight at the house. Then again that is another story.

Just at the time I was taking the hotdogs off of the grill the three kids came rolling in. All of then noticed the cans of baked beans on the fire pit grill and started asking questions about the beans cooking in a can. I reminded them that when you are in the woods you need to be resourceful with the things you have. I also reminded them, we still need a good idea of how to transport the fire wood back to camp later. After that they started chatting away about the things they had seen on their bicycle trip around the camp grounds. Mom told them to save their story for the dinner table and to go to the wash station and get cleaned up for dinner. After their bike ride they all looked like dirty little pigs from all of the dust and dirt they kicked up.

Sitting at the picnic table for dinner and after the dinner blessing was asked, the kids proceeded to tell us about all of the different things they saw. There was the lake with the beach, the small dam for the overflow of water, clean water pump, out houses with a smell, kids play area, baseball field, etc. It seemed like they had never talked that much at the dinner table before. I told the kids that after dinner they will need to take some time and get their sleeping bags and other things organized in their tents, because night time will be coming soon. After that we were going fire wood hauling again.

Well it was time to gather wood. I asked the boys if they had a good idea yet on how to haul some wood. One of them suggested we take the tarp and rope we had and make a sled to load it up and pull on the ground back to camp. We all agreed it was a good idea and away we went. Of course Sis had to come and help this time. After getting back to the old downed trees we began to cut and saw some pieces to put on the makeshift sled for hauling it back to camp. We worked on the wood for a little while and then headed back to camp. The boys were pulling the tarp with Sis and me carrying back what we could. Once we got back to camp the kids went bike riding, with the rule to be back before dark. With the night setting in we all gathered around the camp fire for marshmallows and s'mores. Soon it was bedtime and it seemed like the kids were all asleep pretty fast. The laughing and giggling was short lived, it must have been all that fresh air and work outside. That will do it every time.

After a couple of days it was time to head home. We all started off with a hearty breakfast of sausage, potatoes, and eggs. After that it was time to pack up and head home. I made sure to teach all of the kids how to shut down a camp site. We needed to make sure we put out the fire completely, cleanup all trash, dispose of all uneaten food and other related things. The kids asked if we were going to leave the found fire wood. I said of course that way the next person would be thankful. I looked over at Sis and she was crying her little eyes out. I asked what was wrong and, she said, "She was crying because she did not want to go home". She said she was having too much fun. Go figure she cried when she had to come and now she is crying, because she has to leave. Women!

As I think back on this, what a blessing the Lord gave me. I had the chance to teach my family about several things regarding camping. I also was able to train them in how to set up a proper camp area, tents, fire building, wood hauling and many other related camping items. What a great time we had getting away from the hustle and bustle of our daily lives and enjoying what the Lord has created for us. It was a great opportunity to learn that material things do not matter. The things that the Lord has created, yes even us and each other are what really matters. This camping experience led to many other times we could get together as a family and enjoy what the Lord has created for all of us.

33 Finger Lick 'in Good

It was the year of 1971 and I had just turned fourteen years old. I had went to the county court house and picked up my workers permit. With just getting out of school for the summer I was looking forward to finding a summer job. At that time I was too young to have a driver's license and a car. I did have the old trustworthy bicycle. It did not look like much, but it did get me where I wanted to go.

After a couple of days looking for that job I wound up getting one at the local Kentucky Fried Chicken restaurant. The starting pay was around $1.40 an hour. To a fourteen year old boy this was big money back then. After filling out the required paper work and showing proof of my workers permit, I would be starting the next day. After my interview and receiving the offer of the job, I left and rode all the way home to let my family know that I got the job. I needed to time the route and see how long it would take me to get to work the next day, on my bicycle. Fortunately it only took me about twenty five minutes with my bike to get home. It was hard to get to sleep that night due to the excitement of starting training the next day. Eventually I did fall to sleep for what seemed like a short period of time.

The next day I was up at the crack of dawn. I had been told by my boss to show up at nine a.m. sharp for the first day of training. After getting ready for work, I had a bowl of cereal and a couple of pieces of toast. I packed up a small lunch and away I went. After arriving at work my boss Brian, showed me where I could put my lunch and other items. Brian took me into his office and we went over a few things before he showed me around and introduced me with some of my coworkers. After a little while Brian handed me off to one of the other cooks for training.

Jim the cook that was my trainer showed me where to get clean aprons, where my uniforms would be and then he showed me all of the items in the kitchen. Jim showed me the layout of the food in the cooler. Now it was cooking time. The first thing that I learned was how to bread the chicken. There was an area where you would set the chicken that came out of the cooler. The chicken was already cut into the different types of pieces. In case you did not know it there are eight pieces to a whole chicken. It consisted of two legs, two thighs, two wings and two breast. There were the gizzards and livers, along with the neck bone inside the cavity of the chicken. Before breading the chickens we would take out these items to use at a different time.

Now it was time to bread the chicken. We would take a large bag of flour, which was about twenty five pounds in weight and pour it into a stainless steel tub on the breading station. We then would take a small bag of seasonings and pour it into the flour. After thoroughly mixing the flour and seasonings together, the breading was ready for the chicken. I once asked what was in the seasoning packet and the boss told me that was the secret recipe you would hear about on the television. Well, it looks like I will never know the secret recipe. We then would bread up enough chicken to start the cooking process.

It was now time to start the cooking of the chicken. Along the side of one wall in the kitchen was a row of pressure cookers setting on what was a very long stove. The stove consisted of about sixteen pressure cookers all setting on their own single burner. In all of these cookers there was cooking oil filled to a marked line inside the cooker itself. To fill these with oil, you would take a fifty pound block of shorting and drop it into a large fryer that was sitting next to the stove to melt down the block. This fryer was also used to cook french fries and other related menu items. After the shorting was melted down you would then take a metal container and transfer the warm shorting to the pressure cookers and fill each one to the designated mark. After checking the temperature of the hot oil in the pots you would then start loading the chicken in. When you loaded the cookers with the breaded chicken, there was a certain number of different types and pieces to be put in each cooker. By the time you finished the last pot in the line, it was time to go back to the first pot and attach the lid. After attaching the lids and setting the pressure gages it was time to set the timer. When it came time to unload the pots you would start with number one pot and lift the pressure gage for the steam to be released. Working your way down the line you would do this to each pressure cooker until you got to the last one. After that you would go back to the first pot and remove the lid. You would then work your way down that line until all lids had been remove. Sometimes if you got into a bit of a hurry and remove the lid before most of the steam would be exhausted, the lid would fly out of your hand and the oil would come splashing out. As you can see it would be very easy to get burned while cooking the General's secret. After the chicken was removed and put on draining trays which were then stored in a warming oven waiting to be served.

It had gotten late in the evening and it was time for me to head home. My boss called me into his office and asked how it went. I said that it was something that I never had done before and I enjoyed the chance to work there. He just chuckled and said he received a good report on my working the first day from the other team members. He asked if I had any questions. I said that the only question I had was what was in the secret recipe. He told me if that was known, then it would no longer be a secret. We both laughed and he gave me my work schedule for the rest of the week. After that I left for home on my bicycle. I could not wait to get home and get the smell of that chicken grease off of me. Today sometimes when I go by a restaurant with the smell of chicken grease is in the air, I think back of when I worked at KFC cooking that chicken.

Thinking about this and wondering of what the Lord will have me learn, with my time of being a chicken cook. Does He want me to remember that good hard work will build integrity in me? Does He want me to learn that it is Ok not to know everything, even what is in the secret recipe? Maybe He is telling me that others are watching me, to see if I will be a team player. Or is He reminding me even when someone smells like chicken grease, they may be doing great works for Him. Great now I am hungry for fried chicken.

34 Eight Boys Overnight

With three children all about a year apart it seemed like there was always something going on around our home. If we weren't going to a ball game of some kind, we would be on our way to a band competition, somewhere. It seemed like from the time our children were in junior high and all the way through high school, we were on the road traveling from one sporting event or one band competition all the time. It was a good thing that gas was a little less expensive back then from what it is today. Thank the Lord tires were also lower in price back then.

With our kids being active in several different types of extra-curricular activities, they had made quite a few friends. At times our children would ask to have some of those friends overnight. On one occasion our two boys asked to have some of their friends spend the night. After discussing this with my wife we allowed the boys to invite three of their friends each over. Of course, with eight boys in the house we knew that we would not get much sleep that night. We would always let the kids have their friends over on a Friday night only. Saturday night they would be up to late and then it would be too hard to get them ready for Sunday morning church.

The plan was to go to the grocery store and stock up on extra food items that eight young hungry boys would love to eat. Now this consisted of chips, cereal, milk, soda, snack cakes and just about any other thing you could think of. At that time when the boys were in their teenage years they could go through a mess of groceries, like a swarm of locusts could go through a wheat field. Yes, even the girls at that age could well do a bit of damage also. After returning from the store with what seemed like enough food to feed the US Army, we unpacked the bags and started preparing homemade pizza for all of the eight boys to eat for dinner.

We had just finished putting the extra leaf in the dinner table when the door bell had rang. Upon answering the door we met each of the boy's parents, each time one of them were dropped off and asked for a phone number, in case an emergency came up. It seemed like the parents were happy that they were losing a child for the night. Some thought we were crazy for having that many over at one time. Others thought it was a good idea and was looking forward to the time they could have one of the kid's friends over for a night. But then again that was another story. After all of the boys showed up pizza was served and the feasting for the eight had begun.

After dinner they all went to the boy's rooms for a time of game playing. They would get on the TV and play video games along with other board games. It seemed like the good times for them were on a roll. Every once in a while a couple of them would come out of the room only looking for something to snack on. It seemed like the snacking would go on forever. At times I thought they all had a bottomless pit when it came to trying to fill them up after dinner. It was a good thing that we always made extra pizzas for them to have after dinner. Like they always say, always room for jello, pizza, chips, etc. when you are a teenager. The grazing by those boys seem to of went on well into the night. Sometimes when our daughter would have a group of her friends stay over, they would give the boys a run, in the amount of food they could devour in a night. But then again that is another story.

It was always fun the next day to be around them when they woke up for breakfast. We would fix a ton of flap jacks and sausages. We always hoped for some of the milk to be left in the fridge from the night before. If not, the backup plan of frozen orange juice to mix up was in the freezer. At the breakfast table there was a lot of chatter about who won what game and the planning of staying next Friday night at someone else's home. Soon it was check out time and the parents started to show up to pick up their boys. Our two would always thank us for allowing their friends to stay the night and wanted to know when they could do it again.

As I think back to this time, I relate to what the Lord would have me take from this? Did He want to show me that children are very precious unto Him? Do you need good solid friends to help you take that stroll through life on the earth? Is time with friends you have made, worth more than any material items? Do we realize that Jesus is a friend to us and will walk beside us, if we believe and let Him? Can you say that Jesus is your friend today?

35 Four Men and 21 Boys

It was around the summer of the year of 1985. We had been attending a local church. At that time there were quite a few children in the children's program of the church. There was a gentleman named Preston that wanted to get some of us men together and take the boys from the ages of seven to eleven years old on a weekend campout. With that being said Preston recruited myself and two other gentlemen by the names of Jim and Guy.

It stared about three weeks before the leave date. We had to send home permission slips with the boys, along with other informational sheets, related to the weekend campout. After collecting all signed permission slips, we wound up being able to take twenty one young and eager campers with us. This worked out to a ratio of less than six boys to one adult.

The next phase of the great kid campout went into effect. We needed to fine tents and other related camping items for all of us to go on this camping trip. With that many boys and us four men, we also had to gather enough coolers and food to make it through the two day weekend. After the report of the great kid campout, went before the congregation of the church we had members that were willing to donate all of the camping items and food we needed. The church bus was then reserved and ready to transport the weekend campers to a state campground near to the church.

Shortly after all of the groundwork had been done it was time to get on the bus and head to that campground. Now the state campground of Ely Lake was only about an hour drive from the church. I was glad it did not take us to long to get there. While in route we were able to sing some of the old Christian hymns and children's songs. This seemed to help speed the time of the trip up. I swear that the time was cut in half when we arrived at our site. It was now unload and set up time. Each fellow took a group of young gents and started to set up an area for their tents.

The staging of the camp was completed and it was time to gather for the starting of a campfire. One thing about this trip, was that some boys had never been camping. This gave us men a chance to not only teach the little guys about the Lord, but also a time to teach some of them life skills. After the fire was going it was time to fix supper. With the chore of making dinner we had to set up a four foot by five foot steel plate. This was the same plate that was used in the adult campout trip the last month. Fortunately it had been seasoned very well and if not level, an egg you were trying to fry, would slide right off. After grilling hamburgers, hotdogs, potatoes, and cooking some bake beans it was dinner time. I remember one of the eight year olds, in my group said that he ate before he came and he was not that hungry. I suggested he just try some of the cooked items, because breakfast was a little while away. He must have changed his mind, or he tasted something good off of the grill, because he was going back for seconds.

After dinner time, it was a chance to have a devotion with the boys, around the camp fire. After hearing what kind of lives some of these little ones were facing in the days at home, it made me want to cry. Some of these boys did not have fathers in their lives. Some did not even have mothers in their lives. Some were being raised by their grandparents, or even by someone in a foster home, they lived in. Some of their horror stories would make the hair on your neck stand up. After our devotions and conversations' had ended, Preston asked if any of them wanted to know Jesus. Praise the Lord there were four little ones that accepted Christ as their Savior that evening.

When finishing up with Guy playing the guitar, singing, and some old fashion campfire ghost stories, it was time to hit the sack. Each group of boys went to their assigned tents with their assigned adult. The next morning was a time for breakfast. All four adults had risen before the kids and had a time to have that first cup of coffee and plan out the day's events. There would be a baseball game, swim time, short hike in the woods and other related camping activities. Of course we would start the day out with a time of worship, in our own little service at the camp ground. After the day was winding down we all worked on getting some things packed up and ready to go for the return trip home the next day. That night we had devotions around the campfire again and a couple more boys reached out and received the Lord. We all called that a successful camping trip for Jesus.

The ride home was a lot more quite, then the ride to the camp ground. Most of the boys were sleeping on the ride home. I guess all of that fresh air and exercise, must have worn them out. It also looked like Jim and Preston, had a hard time keeping their eyes open. Upon arrival back at the church and as their rides were there to pick them up, it seemed that the boys had come back alive. There was a lot of chatter amongst them with their parents, about the camping trip.

After all of the camping equipment had been unloaded and everything put in its place, the four of us men prayed and thanked the Lord for the chance to do His will. It make me think of just how Jesus loves the little children in the way He does. How I thank God that I did have some caring parents. After hearing from the mouths of babes, with the trials they endure, I can fully appreciate what the Holy Father does for me and the way he takes care of me. As you think back and ponder on this story, how has Jesus Christ taken care of you? Are you able to fully rely on Him in your future, before He comes back? Are you willing to let Him be the pilot of your ship?

36 Chickens On A Trampoline

As I am getting older there are things that I have seen in my last sixty years on this earth. Now I know that there are others out there, which are older and even younger than I am that have probably seen a whole lot more then I have. The Lord has truly blessed me with a time in this world and I can say I have seen some unusual things. To reflect back and think of these things is a true testament that the Lord does make some unusual things happen.

As a kid I had the chance to see some different, unusual, wild and possibly crazy things. One time I got to see a brother of mine ride a pig. If you have never seen something as funny as someone riding a pig I am sure you would have that picture etched in your mind. There is nothing like a good laugh to keep your sanity, as someone riding a pig. But then again that is all together another story.

One time I was at work running a small waste water treatment plant in Paw Paw, Michigan. It was time to make a round outside on top of the clarifier. As I started up the bottom of the stairs that led to a steel catwalk above the circular clarifier, I heard a weird noise. Not paying too much attention to it I started up the stairs. It was nice to be on the catwalk because sometimes you could see deer, turkeys and other wildlife out in the woods or fields next to the open clarifier. Much to my surprise as I arrived at the top of the stairs was a grey crane setting on the edge of the clarifier. As soon as the crane noticed I was on top of the cat walk he took off in flight and landed in an open field about four hundred yards away.

Another thing that I was able to see while working at the water plant, was a helicopter, trimming trees that were growing along the open areas of the power lines that were close to the water plant. You are probably wondering how a helicopter can cut down trees. It was a very neat mechanical type of operation to see. On a long cable hanging from the chopper was a long steel pole with several circular saw blades which were a pretty good size. When this beast of a saw was running it made quite the sound that was very loud and different. To watch something like this was a real treat for a type of person like myself.

One other time when I made a trip on top of the clarifier I was looking in the sky and seen another helicopter. This helicopter had a large platform attached to one side of it and a person was standing on the platform working on the wires of the huge electrical tower lines running across the field. I bet that guy out on that platform with that chopper flying next to the power line had a hard time getting life insurance for himself. How would you like to explain what kind of work you do to the company wanting to sell you a life insurance policy?

Let me tell you about the chickens. It was a warm sunny afternoon. My wife and I had took a ride to the local Walmart. As we were backing out of the driveway we decided to take the back roads to Wally's World. Living in the rural community that we do, it was about a seventeen mile journey. Driving through the country side and enjoying the view of all of the fruit orchards, corn and blueberry fields in our part of the fruit belt of Michigan we came across a trampoline in the front yard of a house. Much to our surprise as we moved closer to the house, there were about six chickens all on the trampoline. We slowed down a little and was amazed that these chickens were actually jumping up and down a little as they were pecking at the trampoline. I am not sure what they trying to eat that was laying on the bed of that trampoline, or if they were just pecking at it. It sure did look like all six of them were having a good time. If one of them had bounced in the air and did a complete flip, my wife and I probably would have lost it and drove the truck into the ditch laughing so hard. Oh how I wished that I would have had a video camera that day. Yes, God does have a sense of humor.

Now as I go through life and remember back to some of the things that I have seen in my lifetime, I am still amazed when the Lord shows me something I have never seen before. Sometimes we say that it looks like we have seen it all, but we have not. One of these days when our Jesus comes back to gather all of us that are born again and takes us to heaven, I wonder what things we will see there. I am sure that there will be things that we have never dreamed of seeing there. The greatest one, we will see is Jesus and God the Father. As for me, I imagine that my eyes and head will be like that little gopher that pops out of the hole in the ground and is constantly looking around 360 degrees to see what is around him. What a day that will be. Are you ready to see those wonders that are in heaven awaiting us?

37 Working The Races

It was summer time in the year of 1969. We lived in the small town of Millburg, Michigan. There was only a gas station, small grocery store and of course the old time seed and feed company, for the local farmers. A quarter mile outside of town there was a motorcycle race track named the Millburg Speedway.

At the speedway every Saturday night and Sunday afternoon there would be motorcycle races. Being somewhat of a gear head I would try to attend these races as often as I could. It was nice and convenient to get to the speedway, seeing that all I had to do was jump the backyard fence and walk through about three hundred yards of woods and I was there. Now being a kid without a whole lot of money back then, yes I did sneak in without paying.

Now on one of the Sunday afternoon races that I had slipped in through the woods to watch, I went to the concession stand wanting to get something to eat, with the fifty cents I had in my pocket. The older lady that waited on me made the statement to one of her coworkers this is the boy that likes to sneak into the races for free. At that point I had been busted. The lady that had confronted me was one of the owners of the racetrack. At that point I did confess and wanted to apologize for my actions. Of course one of the first things that went through my mind was to run all the way home. Another thing was I am in trouble and I am going to go to jail. After several thoughts of how I was going to be punished for this crime was going through my mind, I heard the owner say that she had to take a minute to think of what she was going to do with me.

What seemed like an eternity of time had passed in that couple of minutes, the owner gave me the sentence of the price to pay for my crime. She told me her name was Janice, and this is what I could do to pay the price of sneaking into the races without paying. Janice said that I could work in the concession stand the rest of the day with her without pay. I quickly took her up on the offer and was willing to do anything to get out of going to jail. Of course Janice had to call my mother and tell her what had happened and let my mom know where I would be the rest of the day. After that I would have that phone call in the back of my mind and wonder the whole time of what the punishment would be when I got home.

The time was getting close to the end when my punishment would be soon completed. Little did I know that the hard part of my punishment for the crime I did was coming up. Janice the owner had shown me where the mop, bucket and other cleaning materials where for cleaning the men's and ladies' restrooms. As you can image there was a lot of activity at a race track with a lot of people attending. Yes it was time to do the solidarity confinement of my sentence. After spending a couple of hours cleaning those bathrooms, I swore to myself, that I would never sneak into a place of business again. I noticed from time to time that Janice had been following up on me while I was in the process of cleaning each bathroom. I was just about done when she showed up and said that she wanted to talk with me and told me to come to the concession stand when I was finished with putting all of the cleaning items away.

As I was walking into the door of the concession stand Janice told me to come into the back room with her. Janice asked if I had learned my lesson about sneaking into the races without paying. She also make comments of how it was not only illegal, but also immoral. Janice reminded me that a young man of integrity and character would not do these types of things. She also sprinkled a little truth of a Christian young person would also not do something like what I did. At the end of our conversation Janice said I did a good job. She asked if I wanted to come and work for her in the concession stand on the weekends there were motorcycle races. I told her that I could do that if it was ok with my mother. She gave me her phone number and told me to call the next day and let her know. Janice also reminded me that I had better not try to sneak into the races again or the next time she might not be so easy on me.

All the way home the thought of the punishment I would receive that had been on my mind all day was going to happen. After the discipline for my crime at home was completed I did work the rest of the summer on weekends at the race track. I was even able to put a little money in my pocket after buying my school clothes and supplies I needed for the new school year.

As I think more about the things that the Lord wants me to learn from this event in my life, I am thankful for the punishment that was given to me. I could have went to jail, or even to a place for young men that do illegal things. When thinking of this, Janice had to be directed by God to see that a young person was in need of guidance in making good life choices. I think to myself today when making those choices in the travels of my life are they God directed or are they Don directed? What kind of choices are you making when blazing a trail with your life today? Is it a choice being directed by the Lord or a choice being directed by something or someone else? When we think of it God does give us that will to make a choice. Will we make the right choice?

38 First Day Of School

It was around that time of the year for school to start. It was early in the morning and all three of the kids had taken their baths and it was time to take them to school. Normally they would all walk to school. Being the first day of school and it was somewhat of a tradition my wife and I would take a vacation day to get the kids off on their way. As we had done in the pass all of us would jump in the car and away to school we would go.

The ride to school always started out with a lot of excitement. We would roll down the windows and turn up the music. Sometimes the kids would say that we were embarrassing them and ask us to please turn down the music. We did remind them and of course mess with their minds when we told them we might sign up as chaperones for the first school dance of the year. Of course they would then get quite and not say too much of anything, after that. As soon as we stopped in front of the school, the doors would fly open and away they went. I guess we had done a good job of embarrassing them to the point where they could not get away from mom and dad fast enough.

After the kids had been dropped off to school then it would be our time. We would go out to breakfast, do some shopping, eat lunch out, catch a matinee, or even head to a local museum for some time together. My wife would sometimes make the comment that she felt guilty about us getting away alone for the day. Of course I would remind her that it was ok for us to have some time to ourselves once in a while. Besides that when the kids got home from school there would be cookies and other treats for them to enjoy. When the children came home from school we would look forward to hearing about how their first day of school had went.

It was a couple of weeks after school had started and we received a call from our son Mike's teacher. Mike was in the seventh grade in middle school. Seventh grade was the time of that tender age of a child when embarrassing them was the cardinal sin; of a parent. Mike had a problem with getting a failing grade in his math class. The teacher had set up a meeting with the both of us the following day after I had gotten off work. When I had come home from work that day we both sat down and talked with Michael to find out why he was getting a failing grade. Of course Mike, said he did not know.

As my wife and I were talking we could not figure out why our son was getting a failing grade in math. We both would help him with his homework every night. The next day came and we arrived at the school to meet with Michael's math teacher. After we had talked with the math teacher, we found out that Mike has not turned in any of his homework assignments for the class. We both assured the teacher that we had helped Mike with his homework and that all assignments were completed. Now Michael had been outside the classroom door while we were having the meeting. My wife asked the teacher if it would be alright for her to come to class with Mike to make sure that he turned in his homework. The teacher thought that would be a good idea. I asked the teacher if I could bring Mike in and confront him on why he did not turn in his, homework. She said that would be great and then, my wife would tell him that she would be in school with him. Well to make a long story short, after about two weeks of my wife hanging out with Mike in school all day, the problem he had in math class, along as any other problems the teachers were having with him, came to an end. Of course when the other two children saw this they walked a straight line themselves.

There is a time that all of our children has embarrassed us as parents. There also is a time as parents when we have embarrassed our children. As I think back at this time in my life I wonder how many times have I embarrassed our Lord. Being one of His children I am sure that I have done things the Lord would not have approved of. As parents, like we do with our kids which we have been blessed with we look pass the embarrassment and love them unconditionally. How much more are we blessed when the Lord looks pass that same type of embarrassment and unconditionally loves us? Have you put yourself in the position of causing the Lord to frown at what you have done? Are you willing to be able to let the Lord forgive that embarrassing time? As a Christian are you doing your assigned homework and turning it into Him? Like Mike we do have that choice of passing or failing. What will be your choice?

39 Outdoor Drive Inn

Some of you may not remember the time of the Outdoor Drive In. The Outdoor Drive In was a place that you could drive your car into and watch a movie on a big screen. That's right, you could set inside your car and watch a couple of movies. Even today the area that I live in still has a couple of outdoor theaters. Sometimes on a Friday or Saturday evening we will drive by and see some cars parked in a line waiting to get in. This brings back memories of going to the drive in with my parents.

Getting ready to go to the Outdoor Drive In was a lot like getting ready to go camping. I can remember packing up the car with some snacks, blankets, lawn chairs and coolers. We would then load up all of us and head to the show. Back when I was younger we had to pay admission for each person in the car. Every once in a while as it was getting a little dark outside you would see a car come in and park and suddenly the trunk would open and a couple of people jumped out. Some people did this so that they did not have to pay the admission to get in. Of course once in a while somebody would get caught and they all would be thrown out of the drive in. After a few years the places of business started to charge by the car no matter how many people where inside it.

The art of finding that perfect place to park at the drive in was a challenge. If you had kids you always wanted a spot, close to the playground area. If you were on a date you wanted that spot away from the playground, concession stand and as many other vehicles as possible. You had to have that kind of spot in case you were able to do some rubber necking with your date. Now if you were in a pickup you wanted that spot where you could back into it to set up some lawn chairs in the back of the bed. Whatever dictated the kind of spot you needed it had to be done before the start of the movie, or everybody there would be unhappy with you driving around with your lights on.

After you had paid the ticket price to get in and had found that perfect place it was time to get everything set up. First order of business was to take the speaker from the pole you parked next to and hang it on the window of your car. Normally there would be two speakers on each pole and if you were lucky no one parked next to you, then you could use the other speaker for yourself. Back then this was called the stereo sound effect. It was always an unwritten rule to try and not park next to someone else. The next step was to set up any lawn chairs you may have brought. With lawn chairs you could almost use these anywhere in the drive in. There was always a few moms in lawn chairs near the playground chatting and watching their children. It was like the local tea spot for the ladies on movie night. Next thing was to get the blankets and pillows ready for the kids when it came time for when they wanted to go to sleep. Soon all was set up for the long night of movies. Sometimes there would be three movies shown and it made for a long night if you stayed the whole time.

It was now starting to get a little dark and the first movie would be starting shortly. We made a run to the concession stand to pick up some popcorn and a couple of Pic's. Some of you may think that Pic's are some kind of a picture or some type of food. The Pic's at the Drive In we picked up back then were a round coiled object, much like the electric element on top of an electric range. We would take these and light them on fire inside the car to keep out the mosquitoes. It seems odd, but they did do the job. After all of the setup and getting ready, it was now movie time. The kids were still playing at the playground and some of the moms were still there having their evening tea time. As it had stared to get darker one by one the playground kids and moms were leaving and going to their cars. The screen had lit up and the cartoons before the show had started. One of the cartoons that I will never forget is that dancing hotdog and it telling us to go to the concession stand to pick one up. We also had the Pic commercial at the beginning to remind us to purchase one at the concession stand.

Of course, with the first movie starting there was always a few late comers showing up and driving around looking for that perfect spot. With the movie starting and all of the kids back at the car looking for something to eat or drink, it was time to set back and enjoy the show. It always seemed like after the kids had consumed their drinks and snacks, mom had to take them to the restrooms. Usually with a short amount of time into the movie the kids would start dozing off to sleep, one by one. Soon after that it was all quite for mom and I to enjoy the silver screen. Before too long my wife and I would have a hard time staying awake to watch the end of the show, at that point we would quietly pack up and head home.

One of the things I think about from going to the Drive In back in the day was the special time we had with our children. With them all being grown and families of their own today, that precious time we had with them is missed greatly. Sometimes I think of how Jesus misses that time we do not spend with Him. We sometimes neglect to go to Him in prayer as much as we should. Sometimes we do not add Him in our decision making for our lives. How much more would we enjoy our time here on earth if we would only take that time to be with Him? I know that I need to spend more time with the Lord, how about you?

40 High School Speech

It was the year of 1970 and the first day of high school for this young freshmen. I had received my list with all of the classes and their room numbers, I had signed up for. The school I went to was a very big high school. There was four hundred and eighty six in my graduating class alone. So if you did the math there were more than fifteen hundred students in this high school. We had to complete certain requirements of various classes before you would receive your graduation diploma. With that being said, one required class was a half semester of some type of speech class. Of course wanting to get the required classes out of the way as early as possible I signed up for a public speaking class, in my freshmen year.

I remember it so clearly that first day in speech class. Our teacher introduced himself as Mr. James. He had said that we were going to start the class out with a little impromptu speech for five minutes from each student. He stated that whoever did not get done today, they would finish up tomorrow. He instructed us to say our name, grade and reason for taking the public speaking class. He also said that he would give us the topic of our speech, when we stood up in front of the class room, prior to starting our speech. With having to give a speech that first day without any preparation made me very nervous. It sure seemed like there was so much nervous tension in the room, you could cut it with a knife.

Suddenly it was time and the instructor picked a student to start the class off. The first person went to the front of the class room and proceeded to tell us their name and other required information. After that Mr. James assigned the topic of how you would feel if you were a rock to the speaker. The student gave their speech while Mr. James started timing them. After that Mr. James picked another person to give a speech on how they would feel if they were a baseball. That speaker gave a very funny speech on that topic and it seemed to have relaxed the entire class.

While I was waiting my turn I started to think this was not going to be too hard after all. It looked like all of the topics were going to be pretty simple. After a couple of other victims had done their speeches in front of the class, Mr. James picked me and it was my time. As my turn had come I was feeling pretty confident in myself and thought I could do this with no problem. On the way to the front of the class I was thinking what kind of object would I be assigned to speak about? I said to myself that I had this in the bag for a good grade.

When standing in front of the class I heard Mr. James say those words. Class, let's change it up a little with the topics we will be speaking about. After hearing these words I shot a look toward the teacher, as he started to give me a topic to speak on. Mr. James said Don, speak to us about the right to freedom of speech. As my heart sank, I could feel my stomach coming up into my throat as I started to talk. Not knowing that much about this topic and wishing that I would have had that required government class before this one, I spoke to the best of my ability on the subject. With the little knowledge I had on the subject, it seemed like it took forever for me to complete the impromptu speech assignment.

After my turn our instructor lectured to us for a couple of minutes about how we may not always be able to be prepared to give a speech on a topic. He suggested that we learn and absorb as much about all things that we can. Mr. James made the statement, no matter how old we get, we will always be learning something we did not know.

Thinking about this time in the past and what I have learned from it is, you never know when you will be thrown a curve ball. Being a believer in Jesus Christ, I do have help with those curve balls when they come my way. The Lord is always there, as the Coach in my life. He leads me in the direction that guides me around those bases and lands me at home plate. The Father is there to tell me when I need to swing for the fences or lay down a bunt. Do you have Him has the leader of you and your team? Can you say that He will be at home plate to greet you with open arms from your run around those bases? So when you are not sure you can hit that curve ball out of the park remember to look to the Coach for the signal to swing away, or lay down a bunt. The Lord's team is the winning team to be on.